ONE + ONE = BLUE

= BLUE

MJ AUCH

Christy Ottaviano Books

HENRY HOLT AND COMPANY • NEW YORK

Henry Holt and Company, LLC
Publishers since 1866
175 Fifth Avenue
New York, New York 10010
mackids.com

Library of Congress Cataloging-in-Publication Data
Auch, Mary Jane.
One plus one equals blue / MJ Auch. — First edition.
pages   cm
"Christy Ottaviano Books."
Summary: Seventh-grader Basil's rank as class loser may be in jeopardy
after meeting a bossy new girl who, like Basil, has synesthesia.
ISBN 978-0-8050-9405-3 (hardcover)
I. Title.
PZ7.A898Oo 2013   [Fic]—dc23   2012027356

First Edition—2013 / Designed by April Ward

Printed in the United States of America by
R. R. Donnelley & Sons Company, Harrisonburg, Virginia

1 3 5 7 9 10 8 6 4 2

For Anna Webman—
Wishing you every happiness.

CHAPTER 1

I'm the biggest loser in the seventh-grade class at Calvin Marshall Middle School. So far, nobody has challenged my position. My class was supposed to be the stars in the lower school this year. Then a notice came around in August that said they were changing everything around because of overcrowding. The lower school would be kindergarten through sixth, and seventh grade would move up to the new middle school with grades eight and nine. My grandmother homeschooled me my whole life until this year, so grade levels didn't mean much to me. Besides, for a bottom-feeder like me, the reorganization was no problem. The lowest point is a secure position—it never changes. But for kids like Joel Mack, the class jock, or Ashleigh Gianelli, the class beauty, missing out on a year of ruling the lower school and dropping to the lowest rung on the middle school ladder was a big shock. Joel, who probably towered over just about everybody in his old school, looks like a fourth-grader here. And Ashleigh is pretty, but she can't compare to the ninth-grade gorgeous girls. Some of them could be in the movies. Honest. I'm not kidding.

I figured out right away that lunch can be the worst period of the day because where you sit says a lot about how important you are. Not a worry for me. Right at the beginning of the school year, I staked out a claim at a small table—actually a desk—in the back corner of the cafeteria, where I could observe what was going on. From my vantage point, I've been watching how the other kids formed groups. It took a couple of weeks for the table arrangements to shake out—three grade levels of every category—the gorgeous girls, the jocks, the brainiacs, the techno-nerds, and the kids who think they've hit the jackpot when they get a D plus. Well, that's sort of a bottom group, and my grades could qualify me for that table. I'm not like them, though, because I'm smart everywhere but in school.

When it was just Gram and me doing lessons together, there were no other kids to compare myself to. We would have long, interesting discussions about whatever subject I was studying. Gram made me feel like I was some kind of genius. Then the first few tests in public school put me pretty much on the bottom of the pile. I didn't want to upset Gram by telling her how bad my grades were, but I knew she would find out when the first report cards went home.

To make things worse, most of the kids in my class had been together since kindergarten, and I didn't know any of them. Having a name like Basil Feeney didn't help me fit in, either. My mother, Carly, named me after an herb. It was the main ingredient in her favorite sauce—pesto—so things could have been a lot worse. Carly dumped me with my grandmother when I was five and ran off to Hollywood to become a star.

I might have been able to overcome the bad grades and the no-friends thing if it hadn't been for my freak-ism. I was even starting to make one friend, Jason Ferris. Jason and I sat next to each other in most of our classes because our last names started with the same letter. We weren't exactly best buddies, but he was the closest thing I'd ever had to a kid friend. For a couple of weeks, Jason and I got along pretty well. I even started sitting with him at a real lunch table once in a while.

Then came the day we were supposed to be correcting each other's math review worksheets. Jason read the problem out loud. "One jar holds 635 marbles, and another jar has 463 marbles. If you put them all together, how many marbles would you have?" He looked up from the paper. "You said 798. It's supposed to be 1,098."

"That's because of three and six both being yellow," I explained. "I get them mixed up a lot. Don't you?"

Jason dipped his chin and peered at me over his glasses.

I should have realized something was wrong, but like an idiot I kept going. "Same thing with one and zero both being white. I mean, there are so many colors. Why couldn't each number get a different one?" This seemed so logical to me. For as long as I could remember, every time I saw a number, it had a color for me. And every time I saw a color that was the exact shade of one of my numbers, it would make me think of that number. It was as normal as breathing, which was why I couldn't understand the look I was getting from Jason.

He sat staring at me, but he didn't have to answer because the bell rang and we went to lunch. At least Jason did. He grabbed his lunch bag and was in line by the door before I could stand up. We weren't allowed to cut ahead, so I didn't see him until I got into the cafeteria. By the time I got my milk, Jason was sitting at a table that was full, so I retreated to my desk-table in the back corner.

I saw Jason talking to the kids around him, then they all laughed. He turned and pointed at me, and they all looked at me and laughed again. I was pretty sure he was talking about me, but I didn't understand what was happening until we got in line to go back to class. The kid in front of me—I think his name was Max— said, "My eight is orange. What color is yours?"

So different people had different colors for their numbers? Was that the reason Jason acted so weird? "Eight is sort of a dark blue-purple," I said. "Orange is five for me."

The kids around us started laughing. When I got on the bus for the trip home, I could tell that everybody knew about my numbers and colors freakism. And for the first time in my life, I realized this wasn't a normal thing that everybody had. I could hear comments coming from all over the bus. By the time we got to my stop, I was convinced I was the only person in the world who saw numbers as colors and colors as numbers.

Gram knew I was bummed the minute I came through the door. "Have a bad day, Basil?" She could read me like a book.

"Yeah, I guess."

"Tell me about it. It always helps me to talk about a problem."

I was just about to open my mouth when she said, "As long as it's not a math problem. You know how bad I am at that."

Of course she would think I was having trouble with one of my subjects. That's when I realized that I'd never talked about my colors and numbers thing with her. I had probably thought about colors when we were doing math worksheets, but I couldn't remember ever saying anything out loud. Why would I? I thought everybody saw it the same way. But now I knew I was the odd one. How would Gram feel if I hit her with the fact that her grandson was an all-out freak? So I didn't tell her.

That's when I stopped trying to make friends in school—not that I'd ever had any real friends. I never saw that many kids when I was homeschooled. Once in a while, Gram and I would get together with the homeschooled kids in Broxburg for something like a fossil field trip to Craig's Creek. There were lots of other get-togethers, but I really hated them. I don't think Gram was too wild about them either, because she never forced me to go. Our friends were all adults, older ones like Gram, who didn't have kids my age.

Giving up on having friends really hadn't been my decision anyway. Kids started making fun of other things about me, like my rooster-tail cowlick and my nose, which takes a slight left turn halfway down my face. Everybody thought I was too weird to hang out with. So from then on, I settled into my position as class loser, and I kept the numbers and colors freakism to myself. I kept everything to myself.

CHAPTER 2

It was the first Monday in October when I walked into the cafeteria and knew right away—my class loser title was at risk. There was a girl sitting at my desk-table who could have been the poster girl for Sunny Daze Thrift Shop. I know this for sure, because I'm their poster boy.

I plopped my milk and lunch bag on the table. "This is my spot," I said.

She looked up at me through glasses that had tiny plastic flowers glued all around the openings. I say openings, because there wasn't any glass in them. "There's plenty of room," she said. "Pull up a chair."

She was inviting me to sit at my own table? I stood

there staring, but that didn't seem to bother her. She was busy picking slices of radish out of what looked like a cream cheese sandwich. "I'm Tenzie Verplank," she said. When I didn't move, she got up and grabbed a chair from the techno-nerd table and plopped it down across from her. "Sit. Stay," she ordered, the way you'd talk to a Labrador retriever.

If I went anywhere else, I'd have to deal with a whole table of strangers, so I did what she said. Our knees bumped together as soon as I sat down. I pulled my chair back. I was facing the wall, which made me uneasy. I'd had enough experience with people slapping "kick me" signs between my shoulder blades to know you never sit with your back to the room. Now the only thing I had to look at was Tenzie.

I concentrated on my lunch. This was a good day—thin slices of roast beef wrapped around pieces of avocado, red and yellow pepper sticks with cucumber dip, and almond cookies with cranberries. Gram says it's important to have lots of color in every meal to make it interesting. Some of the lunches she comes up with could be framed and hung on the wall.

"How come you sit here alone?" Tenzie asked. "No friends?"

"I don't see any friends sitting with you," I said.

"We just moved here," she shot back. "What's your excuse?"

Her eyes were drilling a hole into my forehead. It wasn't that they were unusual looking like green or violet. They were dirty bathwater gray. It was the way she looked out of them, not shy and off to the side like you expect from a new kid.

"You got a name?" she asked.

"Basil."

"Basil like in pesto?"

I glared at her. "Just Basil."

We sat there chewing and ignoring each other for a few minutes. Well, I was ignoring her, but I could feel her staring at me. When she started radish-picking the other half of her sandwich, I sneaked another look at her. I don't know anything about girls' clothes, but I was pretty sure hers wouldn't cut it at the gorgeous girls' table. Tenzie had on this big flowy dress thing, and her skinny arms hung out of the short puffy sleeves like the clapper on a cowbell. The dress was a wild print of blue and orange flowers, the exact colors for my two and five. The flowers practically vibrated in front of my eyes, making it hard for me to look away.

Tenzie took the last bite of her sandwich, wrapped the rejected radishes, and got up. "I'm sitting here tomorrow," she said. "See you then, Pesto." As soon as she left, I slipped into my regular seat, but it didn't feel the same now that my safe loser's spot had been invaded.

I spent the rest of lunch period watching Ashleigh Gianelli study the eighth-grade popular girls' table. The older girls all had hair that was straight and shiny and swung forward when they looked down. Ashleigh must have tried to straighten hers out, but in the steamy heat of the cafeteria, it was starting to curl up again on one side. I thought she looked better with curly hair, even if it wasn't swingy, but what did I know? No matter how much gel goop I used in the morning to plaster down my cowlick, it always broke loose by the time the bus arrived at the school.

When I got to my next class—math—I noticed a bright flash of two and five. Tenzie was sitting in the desk in front of mine. She looked over her shoulder. "Hey, Pesto, you following me around?"

I slid down in my seat, hoping nobody had heard what she called me.

Mrs. Lowe was writing multiplication problems on

the board. "We're going to try something different today," she said. "I'm giving you a chance to show off your multiplication facts. When I call on you, stand up by your desk and solve the problem out loud." She said this like she was doing us a favor. This should have been easy for me, because Gram started teaching me multiplication tables a few years ago. When I looked at the problems on the board now, the colors all ran together. Maybe it was because I was scared to stand up in front of the class to answer.

Mrs. Lowe started by calling on a kid in the first row. Before I could get the numbers into my head, the kid had solved the problem and was back in his seat. Then Mrs. Lowe called on the girl behind him. She was taking a little longer to figure out the problem.

I looked at the clock, trying to estimate how long it would take to get to me. Maybe my turn wouldn't come until tomorrow, and I was pretty sure I felt a bad cold coming on. I coughed. Yep, I could feel those little cold germs multiplying in my throat right now, building whole colonies of misery. I'd have to stay home for sure.

Mrs. Lowe called on the third girl in the fourth row. She was skipping people! Not fair! I coughed again, hoping I could bring the cold on faster and go to the nurse. But my plan backfired. My cough caught Mrs. Lowe's attention. I started chanting in my head. *Don't call on me. Don't call on me.* As Mrs. Lowe raised her hand to point at me, I felt my stomach form a fist around Gram's colorful lunch. Maybe I could throw up right now.

"Basil," she said, "you try this problem."

I tried to focus on the numbers. Thirty-eight times nine. Nine! When Gram and I practiced the multiplication tables at home, I always burned out by the sevens, and Gram never pushed me to go further because she was as confused as me.

I stood up. Mrs. Lowe was tapping the eight and the nine, back and forth. Back and forth. It was almost hypnotizing, watching the chalk bounce from one number to the other. Purple, brown, purple, brown. "Come on, Basil. Eight times nine. You know this."

The purple eight and brown nine danced in front of my eyes, and then the blue two and orange five of Tenzie's dress joined them, flashing in and out. What were the numbers I was supposed to be multiplying? Four times eight? No, there was a nine. A brown nine.

Tenzie's blue two and orange five merged and made brown. "Two plus five is nine," I blurted out. There was an explosion of laughter. I wanted to be invisible again.

The kid next to me snorted and slapped his desk. "You kill me, Pesto." He had heard the name.

"Concentrate, Basil. We're doing multiplication now," Mrs. Lowe said with that fake-patient voice teachers get when they don't want people to know they think you're stupid. "What's eight times nine, Basil?"

Tenzie covered her mouth and leaned back. "Seventy-two," she whispered.

"Seventy-two," I said, and sat down, relieved to have the ordeal over.

But it wasn't over. Everybody was laughing again. Did Tenzie slip me the wrong answer?

"That's right, though you're not finished, Basil," Mrs. Lowe said. "Stand up and do the rest." She was bouncing that piece of chalk again. "Three times nine."

"Twenty-seven," Tenzie whispered. As I parroted the answer, I thought about how seventy-two was green and blue, and twenty-seven was blue first, then green.

"Basil, stay with me here." Mrs. Lowe was saying something about how we had to carry over the seven to the twenty-seven. Tenzie whispered the final answer. "Three hundred and forty-two," I repeated after her.

"Very nice work, Basil." Mrs. Lowe had a maybe-this-kid-isn't-a-total-moron-after-all look on her face.

I could already feel the danger of being a non-loser. Now I'd have to live up to the reputation of giving a right answer. "Or maybe it's three hundred and fifty-four," I said, slipping into my seat. The pressure of high expectations slipped from my shoulders and fractured on the floor around me.

Tenzie turned in her seat and gave me a puzzled look.

I just smiled and shrugged. Tenzie was no threat to my loser status or my desk in the cafeteria. She'd be sitting with the eccentric brainiacs in no time. There were a lot of open spots at that table. She'd fit right in.

CHAPTER 3

I settled into my usual seat on the school bus—front row, window, right behind Mrs. Kenyon, the driver. Nobody ever sat with me, because Mrs. Kenyon would stop the bus if she saw anything even slightly out of line in her rearview mirror.

The first couple of days on the bus, I had tried to hide in the back, but it didn't take me long to figure out that those seats were taken by kids who wanted to be as far away from Mrs. Kenyon as possible. I also learned fast that you could get kicked, poked, and pinched without it showing up in Mrs. Kenyon's rearview mirror. Sitting up front in Mrs. Kenyon's force field had kept my bus trips safe and uneventful.

I stared out the side window as the other kids boarded until I felt somebody plop into the seat next to me. "Hey, Pesto, we're on the same bus. How's that for a coincidence?"

I squeezed as close to the window as I could. Tenzie had wrapped a bright fuchsia poncho thing over her dress. I didn't exactly have a number for that color. The closest thing would be a four on steroids. She was going on about her first day at Calvin Marshall Middle. I didn't answer. Just stared straight ahead.

Mrs. Kenyon gave me a look in her rearview mirror, her eyebrows asking a question that I wasn't going to answer.

I became aware of Tenzie's voice again. "You're not so hot in math, huh?" she was saying. "That's one of my best subjects. I could try to help you with that, but I have a weird way of figuring out math problems. Probably wouldn't do you any good." She stuck her elbow in my side. "Hey, anybody home in there, Pesto? You didn't slip into a coma on me, did you?"

Luckily, we were almost to my stop. I always had a

long ride in to school every morning—about twenty minutes—because I lived near the school and was one of the first kids picked up. But going home, I was one of the first ones dropped off, so I'd get away from Tenzie any second now. I saw the first houses in the development across the road from us, then the bus slowed to a stop.

"Well, nice talking with you, Pesto," Tenzie said, "seeing as how you're such a great conversationalist and all."

She was getting up—getting off at my stop! I stayed in my seat until all the other kids from the development got off. Then I slipped down the steps and ran across the road. I saw Gram working in the vegetable garden. She looked up and waved.

The road was like a demarcation line between centuries. The development across the road was so new, some of the houses didn't have grass in the yards yet, and the trees were all little spindly things. On our side, the big maple in our front yard had a trunk that was two feet thick. Part of our house had been around since the early eighteen hundreds. Every family that had lived there had added on to it, so it had multiple personalities. Even though it was the oldest building in town, it didn't qualify as a landmark because the historical society said it wasn't a good example of any recognizable style of architecture. It was mostly built of rectangles like a regular house, except for the hippie room—a huge dome that was stuck onto the back. It looked like one of those slow-motion explosions that you see in the movies, as if pressure from inside caused the back wall to balloon out bigger and bigger, and then it stopped just before it burst. Unfortunately, it could be seen over the roof of the house, so total strangers were always stopping to ask if they could come in and check it out.

As I was heading for the mailbox, I heard a voice behind me. "Hey, Pesto, do you live in that amazing house? What's that big thing in the back that looks like it's trying to swallow the roof? Can I come in and see it?"

It was Tenzie, of course. I tried to think of a way to get rid of her, but it was too late. She had spotted Gram, who was jabbing sprigs of goldenrod in her hair while she picked vegetables. In the sunshine, the flowers made a bright yellow halo around her head. "Wow, your mom looks really interesting."

"That's my grandmother, and she's weird," I said, "so take off while you still can."

That was a bad choice of words on my part. Tenzie

smiled. "I love weird people." Of course she would. Tenzie grabbed my arm and propelled me toward the garden. Before I had a chance to say anything else, we were face-to-face with Gram.

Tenzie reached out her hand. "Hi, I'm Tenzie Verplank. Our family just moved here. I absolutely adore your house."

Gram lifted her face to the sun. "Isn't this a beautiful, warm fall day, Tenzie? It feels like the summer of '67 when I was in San Francisco. They called it the Summer of Love. That's when I met David, Basil's handsome prince of a grandfather."

I hoped Gram wouldn't launch into one of her embarrassing Summer of Love stories, which I had been hearing my whole life. Grandpa died before I was born. He could have been handsome a hundred years ago, but his pictures showed a scruffy old guy who looked more like a frog than a prince.

Gram picked up her veggie basket. "I'm heading inside to make a snack with these last green tomatoes, Tenzie. Will you join us?"

I glanced at Tenzie, hoping she'd refuse the offer, but she didn't. Of course she wouldn't. She and Gram started toward the house, chattering about gardening. I fell back far enough so I wouldn't be expected to join in the conversation. Then I killed some extra time going to get the mail. As usual, it was nothing but ads and craft catalogues. By the time I went in the back door, Gram had Tenzie helping her make fried green tomatoes. A few slices were already sizzling in the pan. The way the two of them were chatting, you'd think they'd known each other forever.

"Tenzie says she and her family have just moved here, Basil. Won't it be cool to have a friend right across the street?"

Gram had somehow missed the fact that at least a couple dozen potential friends lived in the development across the street, and none of them had ever set foot in our house, even though they all waited at the end of our driveway for the bus every day.

I dropped the mail on the table and headed for my room, which unfortunately was right off the kitchen. The constant conversation came right through my closed door. Tenzie was giving a minute-by-minute account of our school day. Gram must be loving that. All she ever got from me were a few grunts. When I finally got out of school each day, the last thing I wanted to do was relive it.

"Hurry up, Basil," Gram called. "Tenzie and I have scarfed half of the fried green tomatoes already."

"I'm doing my homework," I called back, even though Gram would know I was lying. She opened the door. "You have a guest," she hissed, probably loud enough for Tenzie to hear.

"Guest" didn't sound as bad as "friend." A guest was a temporary thing. Just visiting. Just going to have a quick snack, a whirlwind tour of the house, and leave. I could say something clever like "have a nice life" as I waved good-bye. Even Tenzie ought to pick up on that message.

But I didn't have a chance to say anything. Before I could move, Tenzie slipped by Gram and came into my room, which felt weird, because I'd never had another kid in there. Tenzie went immediately to the big wheel that hung on the far wall. "What's this, Basil?"

"A color wheel," I said.

She started spinning the wheel. "I saw one of these in an art class, but it didn't move. Where did you get it?"

I grabbed the wheel to stop it from moving. "I didn't

make it for spinning fast, just for turning to get different colors to line up with each other."

Tenzie stepped back. "Oh, sorry. But you made it? Why? What's it for?"

I didn't like this. I didn't want anybody messing with my stuff. "It's nothing—just an art project I did a few years ago."

"Your grandmother sure thought of great stuff for homeschool projects."

The color wheel had been my idea, not Gram's, but I let it go. "We're just interested in how colors are made, that's all. Go find Gram. She'll tell you all about it."

Tenzie had moved on to my window, where I had shelves lined up with little bottles of colored water. She picked one up and held it to the light. "What's in these bottles?"

"It's more of the same thing. Come on. Gram's waiting."

"You were mixing colors to see what you came up with. I love that." She said it almost in a whisper. When she set the bottle back on the shelf in the wrong place, I couldn't stop myself from moving it to where it belonged. She tilted her head and gave me a questioning look, so I turned away.

I could feel her moving around the room, looking at all my color stuff. I suddenly realized that my room was like the inside of my brain laid out for anyone to see, except nobody was ever in there but me. When I glanced at the expression on Tenzie's face, I could tell that most kids' rooms probably didn't look like this, and I knew most kids' brains didn't work like mine, either. I couldn't stand having Tenzie in there another second. I didn't want her to know how important this color stuff was to me. It was more than important. It *was* me.

I took hold of her arm and led her out into the kitchen. "Come on. Gram is waiting for us." As soon as we got out, I closed the door and gave it that extra pull that clicked and kept it from opening on its own the way doors do in old houses with slanted floors. We both sat at the table, and Tenzie started in about how delicious the fried tomatoes were. Then Gram had to say that they tasted good because of the almond flour and how we never ate any wheat because she read a book that proved modern wheat is poison, letting Tenzie in on another of our family freakisms. At least Gram wasn't wearing her WHEAT CAN KILL YOU T-shirt with the big red blood spatter all over the front. Gram's chair scraped the floor as she stood to get the last of the fried tomatoes, so that gave me an opening.

"Won't your family wonder where you are?" I asked.

"Nobody's home. But I should call Mom at her office to let her know I got on the bus, seeing as it's my first day." Tenzie pulled out a cell phone from somewhere under the poncho, then fished around in there again and came out with a piece of paper with a phone number on it. "Mrs. Verplank, please. . . . It's Tenzie . . . Ten . . . *T-E-N*, no, *T* as in . . ." She looked around. "Table. *T* as in table, *E-N-Z*. No, *Z* as in . . . never mind. Just tell her that her daughter got home all right."

Tenzie shrugged. "It's a new job for her. The people don't know her yet. I'll have to get her extension tonight."

Listening to Tenzie try to spell her name, I realized for the first time that there was a "ten" in it, which was ridiculous, because ten is white, and white is quiet. It didn't fit her at all. Not only did Tenzie wear a lot of loud colors, but her personality was like the brass section of a band. White would be somebody timid like Miss Chelmski, the assistant in the guidance office, who wrote hall passes when you were late for class.

"Basil? Don't you want a fried green tomato?" Gram nudged my elbow with the plate.

"Sure." I took one and bit into it. I had to admit it was good—crunchy on the outside and juicy on the inside. Most of what Gram made was actually pretty tasty. But I wished I could have a little jolt of genuine junk food once in a while, just enough to give my liver some toxins to filter out so it didn't shrivel up from being underused.

I munched on tomatoes while Gram found out more about Tenzie—not that I cared. Tenzie said they always moved because of her father's career as a TV weather forecaster.

"I didn't know weather forecasters moved around so much," Gram said. "There was a new weatherman on Channel Seven this morning. Was that your dad?"

"That was him," Tenzie said. "And he always gets fired, because he's wrong most of the time."

"Don't all of the TV weather forecasters get the same information from the National Weather Service?" Gram asked.

"I guess so," Tenzie said. "But my dad always has to put his own spin on the facts."

Gram went over to the window. "I see what you mean. He predicted a major thunderstorm for this afternoon, but the other stations all said it would be sunny." Because she's a gardener, Gram surfs all the weather reports to plan her day, so she can weed and plant before the big green blobs of rain move in on the radar.

When I looked at the sky, I had a funny feeling that Mr. Verplank might be right, which made no sense, because there wasn't a cloud in the sky.

Tenzie helped Gram gather the dishes and take them to the sink. "Basil, Tenzie wanted to see the house, so give her a little tour, will you? Show her the hippie room. That's everybody's favorite."

"She probably has to get home, Gram." Judging by Tenzie's taste for the weird, I knew if she ever got a glimpse of the hippie room, she'd be coming over here every day until her dad lost his job.

Tenzie looked at her huge Mickey Mouse watch. "It's early. I have time for a tour."

Of course she'd have time for a tour. I led Tenzie through the center section of the house. Gram could tell you when each room was added on, but they looked pretty ordinary to me—square walls, flat ceilings. Gram had painted them some pretty wild colors though, which Tenzie picked right up on.

"I'd love to live in a house like this," Tenzie said.

"There are only two kinds of houses on our street, and they're just a mirror image of each other. They call the development Elegant Acres, for Pete's sake. How embarrassing is that?"

I nodded. Gram was against the construction of Elegant Acres from the minute she heard about it because she liked living out in the country, away from other houses. She even went to a town meeting to protest the development, but it didn't do any good. When the houses were skeletons with no outside walls, I used to climb their stairs to look at the view from the second floor. You could see the town in the valley and the hills way beyond that. Our house didn't have an upstairs, and we were surrounded by trees, so we couldn't see off into the distance. The view was the only thing I envied about Elegant Acres.

When I led Tenzie into the small library, she went nuts. "Purple walls! We have to move around so much, we never can have any interesting colors."

"What does moving have to do with your walls?" I asked.

Tenzie picked up one of Gram's small stained-glass sculptures and held it up to a window to let the light shine through it. "We need to worry about what the next owners will want, so we have to use what the TV design shows call neutrals—things like custard, vanilla, and sugar cookie. Great for eating, but boring for colors. So is this the hippie room?"

"Yes," I lied, because I couldn't stand another minute of the home decorating discussion. "So that's the end of the tour." I steered her back toward the kitchen.

Gram looked up from washing dishes. "That was quick. What did you think of the hippie room, Tenzie?"

"Beautiful," Tenzie said. "I love purple."

"Purple?" Gram dried her hands on a dish towel and raised her eyebrows at me. "Basil must have given you the twenty-five-cent version of the tour. Follow me, Tenzie. I'll give you the full ten-dollar lollapalooza."

As I watched them leave the kitchen together, I knew I was doomed.

CHAPTER 4

Even though you can see the hippie room from the road, you don't get how big it is until you walk into it. When Tenzie looked up, her mouth dropped open. "Wow."

"This type of construction is called a geodesic dome," Gram explained. "It's over twenty feet high at the center. It was built by a hippie couple back in the sixties. That's where the room got its name."

Tenzie was walking around staring up at the walls. They were made of triangles. Some were wood painted with a bright silver metallic paint, and others were all colors of stained glass, which Gram added to over the years every time one of the wood pieces rotted out. There was a steel frame made entirely of triangles that kept the whole thing from collapsing.

"The loft on the far side of the room is where I do my stained-glass work," Gram said. "The long table over here is where I silk-screen fabric designs, and there's my floor loom for weaving."

"Wow," Tenzie said again. For a smart kid, she had a pretty limited vocabulary.

I was so used to being in this room, I forgot how amazing it was. The afternoon sun slanted through the stained glass, setting the silver triangles ablaze with four, eight, two, and seven, and dozens of colors in between that I didn't have numbers for. Sun catchers, which Gram made from long strings of glass shapes linked together with silver chains, hung from high up and slowly twisted, sending arcs of colored light racing across the floor. In bright sun like this, the room put my brain on such overload I could barely hold a thought in my head.

Gram took Tenzie around the room, showing her the various projects she had going. That's how Gram earned money, by selling her fabric and stained-glass designs from her website. Even though Gram tended to be disorganized, she had managed to keep her small business going well enough to support us. Lately, she seemed to be sending out more orders than ever.

The cell phone rang in the kitchen, and Gram ran to answer it. She could never remember to keep it in her pocket.

That's when I looked over at Tenzie and realized she was crying. I didn't know what to say. I hadn't cried since I was a little kid. This would be the hitch with having a friend because it would be my responsibility to ask what was wrong and try to make it better, wouldn't it? I decided to turn away and hope that Gram's phone conversation would be short and she'd be back to handle this before it got embarrassing.

Then Tenzie made a loud choking sound. She had her hand over her mouth, and her cheeks were glassy with tears. "You're so lucky."

"Me? Why?"

"You live in this mind-boggling place. It can look just the way you and your grandmother want it." Tenzie quickly wiped her eyes. "You don't know how good you have it, Pesto." She went over to a bookshelf and picked up a picture in a frame. "Who's this?"

Ordinarily I would have made something up, but I was set off balance by Tenzie's crying and quick recovery. "It's me and Carly—my mother—when I was little," I said.

"She's beautiful and looks so young for a mother. Where is she now? At work?"

"No. She's gone," I said.

Tenzie looked up, startled.

"No, not that kind of gone. She just left—probably not long after that picture was taken. Took off to Hollywood to become an actress."

"Really?" Tenzie wiped the dust from the glass and studied the picture more closely. "Have I ever seen her in anything?"

"Not unless you get LA used-car commercials on your TV. She's done a couple of those. We haven't heard from her in a while."

"It must be fun to go visit her in Hollywood, though." Tenzie carefully replaced the picture on the shelf. "Where's your father?"

"Never met him." I didn't want to get into my family stuff with Tenzie. Then there was a flash of light, followed by a loud boom that set the sun catchers quivering. Just as I noticed that there was no sun left for them to catch, the dome was pelted with rain. I was saved.

Gram appeared in the doorway. "Looks as if your father was right this time, Tenzie."

"Yeah," Tenzie said. "Maybe he's finally getting the hang of this meteorology business." She grinned at me. "We might even get to do some wall painting for a change."

For a storm that wasn't supposed to happen, the rain put on a spectacular show. There was lightning that crackled all the way to the ground followed by one clap of thunder after another.

"I bet Dad is really enjoying this," Tenzie said. "He loves weather extremes. The last place we lived was San Jose, where it was in the seventies and sunny almost every day. Dad got so bored, he started making things up for his weather report. Naturally, he got fired."

A sudden stream of water splatted on the floor, then another and another. "Grab the pans, Basil," Gram shouted. She kept a supply of old dented thrift shop pots and pans in the corner of the hippie room, because every time it rained, the dome leaked something fierce. The three of us ran around the room sliding pots under the leaks.

The sound of the pans catching rain was almost musical. The bigger the pot, the lower the note, and each leak had its own tempo of drips, so there was a lot of syncopation going on. Soon we had an orchestra of nine pans in strategic places catching water.

Gram grabbed a small African drum called a *djembe* from under her stained-glass worktable and started beating her own rhythm on it. "I use the drum to unwind when I've been working on a glass project that sets my nerves on edge," she called over the din. "You can actually get your own pulse to speed up or slow down with these things. There are more drums under there. Help yourself, Tenzie. Drumming isn't meant to be a solitary thing."

Tenzie pulled out my favorite drum and started in, following Gram's rhythm as if she had been drumming all her life. "This is amazing," she said, throwing back her head and laughing.

Gram's eyes were closed now, and she slipped into her own little world. I knew that feeling, where the cadence of the drum carried you away somewhere. But I wasn't being carried away anywhere. I was watching from the outside while my grandmother and my friend . . . no, guest . . . bonded without me. First Tenzie had taken over my desk in the cafeteria, then she had invaded my seat on the bus. Now she was squeezing herself into my family.

And I didn't like it.

CHAPTER 5

I woke up the next morning planning how to avoid Tenzie. I must have been working it out in my sleep because the strategy was all laid out for me. Step one— avoid getting on the school bus. That would give me fifteen minutes of walking in silence instead of an end- less ride listening to Tenzie. The smell of bacon was wafting under my door. Gram looked up from the skil- let. "You're up without being called. What's the occasion?"

"I need an early start today. I've decided to walk to school from now on."

Gram grabbed a couple of eggs from a bowl on the counter. That meant they were brand-new from our hens this morning. "Really. I'm impressed. I usually have to hound you into getting any exercise at all."

I snitched a piece of bacon from the skillet, licking my slightly burned fingers. "Well, that's just it. Yesterday we had a lecture in health class about that very thing, exercise. We're supposed to get at least a half hour a day. By walking to school, I get half of that, and the other half walking home." I chewed my first crunchy bite of bacon, surprised that I could come up with such a reasonable story without even thinking about it. I'd have to try this making-plans-while-sleeping thing more often.

"I hate to spoil your healthy project," Gram said. "But I think I need to fill out some permission slip rigmarole to allow you to walk. I'll get whatever it is today so you can start tomorrow."

Rats! Apparently my dream planner didn't know the school rules. Okay. Plan B. I put down the bacon and clutched at my stomach. "I don't think I can go to school after all. I'm sick."

Gram felt my forehead. "How can you be excited about walking to school one second and sick the next?"

"It came on suddenly." I moaned softly for effect. "There's something going around that sneaks up on you fast. They call it the boo! flu." Wow, that was a good one. Instant rhyming! I gave myself a mental high five, which for me was a high orange.

I didn't have time to see Gram's reaction because she went to answer the doorbell. It was Tenzie. "Basil is going to miss the bus if he doesn't hurry."

Gram looked back at me. "He seems to be under the weather this morning, Tenzie. Says he's coming down with that boo! flu that's going around."

Tenzie came into the kitchen. She was wearing normal-looking jeans, but her shirt had wide green and purple stripes so bright that their numbers—seven and eight—seemed to bounce against each other. "What's going around?"

"The boo! flu," Gram said. "Basil says it strikes very suddenly."

Tenzie peered closely at me. "Oh, yeah, I see the symptoms. It does something to your eyes. Gives you a sneaky, weasely-eyed look."

I glared at her, but she kept talking. "Best thing about the boo! flu is that it leaves as fast as it starts. And it only lasts about a half hour. Nobody's staying out of school for it. C'mon, Pesto. The bus isn't going to wait forever." She grabbed my arm and pulled me to the door, just in time to see the bus disappear around the curve.

"Well, looks as if you'll get your wish to walk to school after all," Gram said.

Walking to school with Tenzie would be even worse than a bus ride with her. At least on the bus I could pretend to fall asleep. "But we can't walk, Gram. We don't have all the paperwork, remember? Can't you drive us?"

"I'd be happy to give you a lift, dear, but the truck was making a funny sound yesterday, so I took the carburetor apart, and when I put it back together, I had a few extra parts left over. I'll figure it out, but could either one of your parents drive you and Basil in, Tenzie?"

"No, ma'am, they leave the house before I do."

"Then we'll just play dumb about the permission slip," Gram said. "I can't stand that bureaucratic nonsense anyway. You might as well sit down and relax for a while, though. If you leave now, you might arrive ahead of the buses. Tenzie, I was just about to scramble a bunch of our fresh-laid eggs for Basil. Would you like some?"

"You mean they just came out of a hen?" Tenzie asked.

"No, we get ours out of a cow," I mumbled.

Tenzie was making a big deal about the eggs. "Wow, you have your own chickens? Look how the yolks are bright orange. Not like the pale yellow yolks from the supermarket. Do you have to cook them differently?"

"You break them into a bowl and beat them up," I said. "It's scrambled eggs, not a science fair project. You two have fun with your cooking class. I'm out of here."

They both looked up, surprised to see that somebody else was in the room. "Be sure to walk facing the traffic, Basil," Gram said. "Or is it with the traffic? I never can remember. I can look it up fast on the Internet."

"It's facing the traffic, Gram. With the traffic is for bikes. See you later!" I took off like a shot, planning to put a lot of distance between me and Tenzie before she started out.

I hadn't gotten halfway to school before Tenzie was by my side. "A grandmother who knows how to cook and take a carburetor apart. She's awesome."

"Yeah, well, a three-year-old can take one apart," I said. "Putting it back together with a couple of pieces left over doesn't make you a mechanic. Gram may be able to weld sculptures, but she doesn't know anything about engines."

We were walking so fast, I was starting to break a sweat and get too breathless to talk, but Tenzie was doing fine. As long as I couldn't lose her, I decided to slow down.

"You mean she made those cool metal dragons out in her garden?"

"Yeah, she started out making a metal scarecrow, then got carried away. She's even sold a few of them on eBay. Only to people who can come pick them up, though. They're too big to ship."

We were passing a field of goldenrod and wild asters. I knew what they were because for one of my homeschool science lessons, Gram and I had walked for miles identifying wildflowers and weeds, and writing down their names in a notebook.

This field had fountains of threes, sixes, and eights spurting up all over the place. It was one of the few places I could see the difference between my yellows for three and six. The freshly blooming goldenrod was clear yellow, like my three. But the older drying-out blooms were more like yellow mustard, and that was my color for six. I was so lost in my color thoughts, I had missed what Tenzie was talking about.

"So are you going to answer me or not?"

"Answer what?"

She let out a sharp sigh. "Pesto, you can be exasperating. I asked you why you didn't want to go to school today."

Maybe if she hadn't called me Pesto, I would have been kinder. Or maybe not. I'm usually honest, which is my best quality—and also my worst. Anyway, the truth popped into my head, and I said it out loud. "I was trying to avoid you."

All she said was, "Oh." I wish I hadn't looked at her because I saw her eyes flicker for a second, then the sparkle went out of them. She had seemed so sure of herself, it had never crossed my mind that she could be hurt by something I said.

I was about to take it back when she jutted out her chin. "Your loss, Pesto." She took off running, leaving me standing there.

I started out fast, but slowed my pace because I didn't want to get to school before the buses arrived. Then it would be just Tenzie and me and a handful of other walkers waiting for the doors to be unlocked.

I felt bad about being mean to Tenzie. But I had to, didn't I? Because she was going to be hanging around my house all the time unless I did something to get rid of her. And she sure wasn't good at taking subtle hints—or even obvious ones. This was the trouble with having friends. They made life complicated. It was much simpler to be a loner—a loser loner.

After I crossed the intersection at the edge of town, several buses passed me. And by the time I reached the school, the bus loop was full. I didn't see any sign of Tenzie, not that I was looking for her. And I didn't see her all morning, which wasn't surprising, because we wouldn't have any classes together until math after lunch.

Lunch! I knew I'd have to see her there. Would she have staked a claim to my desk-table? If she had, where would I sit? When I got to the cafeteria, I didn't have to worry about that because my spot was empty. I slid into my seat, with my back to the wall the way I liked it.

I didn't open my lunch because my stomach felt funny. Maybe I was sick after all. Maybe I should have stayed home. Then, even in all the colors of the cafeteria, a vibrating seven caught my eye coming in the entrance. Tenzie didn't look at me. She walked right over and took the only empty seat at the eighth-grade gorgeous girls' table. I couldn't believe it. Even other eighth-grade girls couldn't sit there unless they were cheerleaders or some other important person.

Tenzie said something to them as she sat down, but nobody answered her. They didn't notice she was there. She was like a flea landing on an elephant. Tenzie said something else that caught their attention. Then the prettiest one made a remark, and they all laughed. Tenzie's face turned bright red, but she smiled and said something back. I wished I could read lips. This time the whole group laughed so loud, people at other tables were turning to look. At first I hoped maybe Tenzie had told a joke, but the way she was skootching down in her seat, I knew they were laughing at her.

I thought about going over to rescue her. I could say something like, "I have some fried green tomatoes at my table that I'm not going to eat. You want them?" That would work. She loved Gram's tomatoes.

But when I played the rest of the scene in my mind, one of the girls would say something like "Oh, look! It's Prince Charming," and the rest of them would think that was hysterically funny. I could picture myself slinking back to my desk-table, humiliated. No, I couldn't do that. The GGs were all laughing now. The one doing most of the talking had an ugly sneer on her face, making me wonder why I had thought they were all so pretty.

Then Tenzie got up and looked right at me. She was coming toward me, dragging the spotlight along with her. I grabbed my backpack and plopped it in the middle of the desk, then stood my cafeteria tray up against it to make a barrier that I could hide behind. I waited for her to get to me—braced myself for hearing her call me that awful name—Pesto. But nothing happened.

When I finally peeked over the edge of my tray fort, Tenzie was gone. Weird.

Even weirder, when I got to math class, Tenzie's seat was empty. Where could she go in the middle of the day?

Mrs. Lowe called on me once, smiling as if she expected me to give the right answer the way I had yesterday. Without Tenzie prompting me, I didn't have a clue, so I just shrugged and gave my usual answer, "I don't know."

Mrs. Lowe's face took on the old indifferent look she had always given me before my sudden flash of brilliance.

As I left school for the day, I considered walking home to avoid Tenzie, but then I remembered I had a package that was supposed to arrive, and I needed to get home fast so I could be waiting for the UPS man. It was a birthday present for Gram, and I didn't want her getting into it by mistake, or accidentally on purpose. I got in line for my bus.

I wouldn't have to see Tenzie anyway. A school bus had a lot of seats. No reason we'd have to sit together. But what if she was already in my seat? Then I'd have to sit farther back toward the danger zone.

As I climbed the steps, I saw that my seat was empty. Good! I slid in behind Mrs. Kenyon and looked up at her rearview mirror. I could see all the seats on my side of the bus, and Tenzie wasn't in any of them, not that it mattered, as long as she wasn't sitting with me. Then I got up and stretched, turning around so I could check out the other side of the bus. Tenzie wasn't there, either. I looked toward the school. Two more stragglers ran to get on, and Mrs. Kenyon closed the door.

Had Tenzie walked home? I watched the other side of the road as we headed out. That was the side she should be walking on. All I saw was a dog and a squirrel. No kids. No Tenzie. Not that I was worried about her. Tenzie Verplank could take care of herself. Besides, she wasn't my problem.

CHAPTER

6

Gram was busy welding a new sculpture in the back-yard, so she didn't even see the school bus. I went into the house, dumped my backpack, snitched some wrapping paper and tape from Gram's stash, and put it in my room before going out on the front porch steps to wait for the UPS truck.

I looked across the street to Elegant Acres. Even though tons of kids got off at our stop, I didn't see any of them outside. I wondered if Tenzie was home. I had no idea which house she lived in. I looked down the road toward school. Maybe she'd been walking on the wrong side of the road and I missed seeing her. I'd have to keep glancing that way so I could duck inside if she came along.

I knew I'd have to face Tenzie sooner or later, and I didn't know what to say to her. Well, I wouldn't say anything at all. Our fight wasn't my fault. I just told her the truth. Nothing wrong with that. And it wasn't a fight anyway. It was just a . . . nothing. It was nothing. I heard a door slam. One of the Elegant Acres girls came out of her house and got into the family van in the driveway. It wasn't Tenzie. There was another slam, and the mother came out and got in the van, and they drove out of the development and down the road.

Then I saw the UPS truck coming. I ran out to meet Fred, the driver, when he pulled up in our driveway. "Hey, Basil, what did you order this time? Something good?" He leaned out and handed me the package.

"It's a birthday present for Gram—a board game called Truth Detector."

"Truth Detector? I've never heard of that one."

"It was her favorite game when she was a kid," I said. "I found it on eBay."

"You really put some thought into that gift," Fred said. "I bet your grandmother will love it." He waved and took off down the road.

Fred didn't know the half of it. I had done an online search on the game and found out there were a few different versions. Then I had to figure out which one was around when Gram was a kid. It had taken a couple of months before the right game in good shape showed up on eBay. The description said it was like new and had all its parts. I barely found it in time for her birthday.

I ran back into my room to look it over. The box had pictures of all the murder suspects around the edge, and the art was great, just the way Gram had described it. I peeked out the window and saw Gram heading for the house, so I wrapped it fast. I wasn't good at wrapping, even when I took my time, so I messed it up pretty bad. I never could get the corners right with those diagonal folds. But it was what was inside that counted. I shoved the present and wrapping stuff under my bed and slid into my seat at the kitchen table just before Gram came in.

"Hi, Basil. How was school?" Gram was still wearing her welder's mask tilted up on her head, which made her look like Darth Vader on a coffee break.

"Okay," I said.

"Oh, come on. Any day you wake up alive is at

least an okay. You must have had something special happen."

I shrugged.

"For instance"—Gram pulled out a chair and sat down—"I found some great stuff at the dump. Somebody threw out a whole bunch of metal parts that make perfect bird beaks. I just made a five-foot-tall crow. I have enough beak parts for a whole flock of crows."

"A murder," I said.

"What?" Gram looked startled.

"The crows. A murder of crows. A scold of jays. A wake of buzzards."

Gram grinned. "Ah, yes. 'An exultation of larks' is my favorite."

"But getting back to murder." I stood up. "Wait here, I'll be right back." I had been planning to give her the game after dinner, but I couldn't resist having such a perfect opening. I grabbed the game from my room and placed it on the table with a flourish. "Ta-da! Happy birthday!"

"For heaven's sake! Is today my birthday?"

"Isn't that why you baked the pecan crust cheesecake that's on top of the refrigerator?"

Gram loved birthdays—especially her own. She was already tearing into the paper, which was why it didn't matter if I did a sloppy job on the wrapping. Gram was as impatient as a little kid when she opened presents.

When she saw the game box, she put both hands over her mouth. "Basil, this is exactly like the one I had when I was a kid. Where did you ever find it?"

"I searched online."

"I never would have thought to look for this game. You're much better at Internet searches than I am." She had taken out the heavy cardboard cards with the suspects' pictures on them. "Oh, look. These were my favorites—the actress and the singer." She put one of the cards on the plastic Truth Detector, then put a stylus through a hole in the card. The needle pointed to the side that said "False," and a bell went off.

"Wow, they must have put batteries in it," I said.

"Doesn't need any," Gram said. "That's the great thing about these old games. They all operate with mechanics. Oh, we have to play this. It's so much fun."

"Let's go!" I slid into the seat across from her and started dividing the suspect cards between us.

Gram put out her hand to stop me. "This game is even more fun with more people. Why don't you ask

Tenzie to come over? We can have some cake afterward. It'll be a real birthday party."

No way I was letting that happen. "I don't know Tenzie's phone number."

Gram rummaged around on the kitchen counter and came up with a piece of paper. "Here. She wrote down her address. Eleven Tasteful Lane. Why don't you go over there and invite her to come?"

"She's probably doing homework, Gram."

"Oh, I suppose you're right."

I was going to let it drop, but Gram looked so disappointed I couldn't. "That's okay. I'll go see if I can find her."

I hadn't walked through Elegant Acres since the first people moved in. I knew the houses were alike on the inside, because they had identical skeletons when they were being built, but I was surprised that nothing made them different on the outside, either. Gram was disgusted that they had only three colors of siding—all shades of beige. And she had heard that the residents had to pick from an approved list of bushes and flowers. "And no vegetable gardens or chickens allowed," Gram had grumbled. "Can you imagine being forbidden to grow your own food on your own land? Why do people put up with that?"

Walking down Fashionable Road, I figured nobody cared about gardens or chickens, because nobody was outside anyway, not even on the little front porches that each house had. I passed Stylish Street and Handsome Way, and was ready to give up when I came to Tasteful Lane. I started looking for number eleven—made of two ones—a double-white number. And the beige of the houses was such a dull color it didn't even deserve a number. A white number on a beige house couldn't be more boring.

I found number eleven and started walking up the driveway. That's when I saw Tenzie sitting on the porch reading. I wanted to hide, but the only tree in her yard had a pencil-thin trunk. I had been planning to ring the doorbell after I had figured out what to say.

Tenzie looked up from her book. "What are you doing here, Pesto?"

"Just passing by," I croaked.

She raised her eyebrows. "Yeah, right. A lot of people pass by here on their way to nowhere."

As I got closer to the house, I could see why most

people didn't use their porches. This one was only wide enough for one chair if you sat in it sideways, because otherwise, your knees would be jammed against the railing. "I, um, came to invite you . . . I mean Gram sent me to invite you to her birthday party."

Tenzie's eyes lit up. "Great! I love parties. When is it?"

"Right now," I said.

"Well, thanks for the advance notice. I don't have a present or a card or anything."

"That's okay. It's not that kind of a party."

"Wait here," she said. "I have to leave a note for my parents."

I sat in the sideways chair and looked around. I couldn't see into Tenzie's house because they had blinds on the windows—beige blinds. All the houses had them, and every one of them had its beige blinds drawn so the people couldn't see anything outside. No wonder they called them blinds. Even all the upstairs windows had blinds blocking the beautiful views.

When Tenzie came out, she had a bracelet of bright-colored glass beads. "Do you think your grandmother would like this? I made it."

"I guess," I said. "But you don't have to—"

"I know. I just want to give her something. I made this for my mother for Mother's Day, but she never wore it, so she won't miss it. Come on, let's go." She bounded off the porch and headed out toward my house.

"Where are all the kids who live around here?" I asked, when I finally caught up to her.

Tenzie shrugged. "I don't know. They weren't even outside on the weekend. Probably playing video games or watching TV."

"I don't have any video games," I said.

"I have a lot of them," Tenzie said. "Well, my father got them for me, but he's the one who plays them. They seem like a waste of time to me. You can spend hours and have nothing to show for it."

That was something we agreed about. Maybe there were other things we had in common. I'd known her for only one day. Was that even possible? Only one day had gone by since Tenzie dive-bombed into my life?

"What happened to you in school today?" I asked. "You weren't in math class, and you weren't on the bus."

Tenzie kept walking, staring straight ahead. "I came home."

"What do you mean? You left early? Did you call your mother to come get you?"

"Nope. I left the cafeteria and walked out the side door."

"But don't they lock the doors after everybody gets in?"

"They're only locked from the outside, silly. They have to open from the inside in case there's a fire or something."

"Didn't the school call your house?" I couldn't believe this. They made it sound as if alarms would ring and the FBI would swoop in and capture any kid who dared to sneak out of school. Tenzie didn't even sneak. She walked.

"Nope. Nobody knew that I left. Nobody noticed, and nobody cared."

We walked along in silence. Tenzie didn't mention what happened in the cafeteria, and I sure wasn't going to bring it up. But guilt hung over my head all the way to my house.

Gram greeted Tenzie like an old friend. "So good to see you, Tenzie. I've set up the game that Basil gave me for my birthday. You're going to love it. And afterward we'll have some cheesecake."

Tenzie handed her the bracelet. "Happy birthday,

Gram." When had she started calling her that? What, she had no grandmother of her own?

Gram's face lit up. "Oh, this is gorgeous, Tenzie. Thank you."

"I made it myself," Tenzie said.

"Yeah, she made it for her mother on Mother's Day," I mumbled.

Tenzie blushed, and Gram looked up. "Made it yourself? My, you have wonderful color sense." Gram hadn't heard my dig at Tenzie, but I felt kind of bad for saying it anyway.

Gram was holding the bracelet up to the window so the sunshine made it sparkle. "Excuse me for a minute, Tenzie. I have the perfect dress to go with this bracelet. I'll go change."

Tenzie and I didn't talk while Gram was out of the room. She looked through the suspect cards for the game, inspecting them as if they were the most fascinating things in the world. I read the directions on the inside of the box, then put the Truth Detector facedown on the table. I shuffled all six Guilty cards and put one into the back of the Truth Detector without peeking. "Okay, the murderer has been chosen," I said.

I couldn't wait to start the game to find out who it was. Gram was a real board-game freak, so if this was her favorite, it must be fantastic.

Gram burst back into the kitchen wearing a fancy dress with rows of bright colored ribbons—mostly two, five, and eight—sewn all around the full skirt. When Gram wasn't wearing jeans, she often wore long skirts. She said they were comfortable and reminded her of the old hippie days. But this was fancier than anything I'd ever seen her in. I wondered if it could have been her wedding dress.

"Look! The bracelet has the exact colors of the ribbons, Tenzie. Couldn't be more perfect if you made it to order." Gram twirled around like a model, holding up the arm with the bracelet.

"I got the game all ready, Gram," I said. "Let's play."

Gram came around my chair and put her hands on my shoulders. "I'm dying to play the game, Basil, but can we hold off for just a few minutes? I think I have the same colors as these beads in stained glass, and I want to show Tenzie. We'll be right back."

I was impatient to start, but I spent the time sorting all the cards and getting everything set up. I also read through all the clue cards, so I'd know what to look for.

They had things like "big eyes," "thick lips," and "bushy eyebrows." When Gram and Tenzie still weren't back, I started with a clue card, then lined up all the suspect cards that fit the description. I wasn't really cheating. I was just trying to make up for all the years that Gram had played the game without me.

After I had gone through all the clue cards and matched the suspects with them, I looked at the kitchen clock. They had been gone for twenty-five minutes. What was going on? How long did it take to look at a few stupid pieces of stained glass? I went out to the hippie room, and my worst fears were confirmed. Gram had started Tenzie working on a stained-glass project.

"Are we going to play Truth Detector or what?" I said, not even trying to hide the fact that I was ticked off.

Gram looked up. "Oh, you know how I get distracted in my studio, Basil. When we looked at the glass in my scrap box, I had Tenzie pick out a few pieces to make a sun catcher. It won't take long."

"I know how long it takes to make a sun catcher," I said. "I've made dozens of them. Even if you use scraps so you don't have to cut the glass, you have to grind the edges smooth, then rub copper foil all around each piece, then solder all the parts together. We'll never get to the game."

Gram stood up. "I'm sorry, Basil. You're right. We'll stop now, and Tenzie can come back tomorrow and work on her project. In fact, we can spread it out over a number of days."

Tenzie coming to our house over a number of days? No way! "Just go ahead and finish the project," I said. "We can play the game another time."

"Well, if you're sure . . ." Gram was asking permission, but she had already sat down, so she wasn't very convincing.

"Oh, yeah. I'm definitely sure." What I didn't say was that the "we" who could play the game another time would be Gram and me. Not Tenzie. If I had my way, Tenzie was never getting into my house again. She could go visit her own grandmother and leave mine alone.

I went back to the kitchen and decided to play the game by myself.

I turned over clue cards and interrogated witnesses. It took quite a long time before I was ready to make an arrest. But when I did, I had guessed wrong. It was no fun playing this game by yourself. Besides, the main reason for getting the present in the first place was to see Gram enjoying the game she had loved as a kid.

Finally the two of them came back from the studio. Tenzie was holding the sun catcher she had made. It was pretty, but I didn't tell her so. Gram glanced at the clock. "The time got away from me. We'd better have some cake now."

"Yes, I told my parents I'd be home by five-thirty," Tenzie said.

So Gram cut the cheesecake, and we each had a piece. Somehow it didn't taste as good as it usually did, which went along with the rest of the birthday celebration. After Tenzie left, I said, "Why did you have to give Tenzie a stained-glass lesson instead of playing the game? And why did you make such a big deal over that stupid bracelet? She didn't even make it for you. She gave it to her mother for Mother's Day."

"Yes," Gram said. "I heard you say that the first time. And I figured if Tenzie was willing to give it away, the gift couldn't have meant much to her mother. I have a feeling Tenzie doesn't get much notice at home. That's why I wanted to make her feel special today."

"That's crazy. Tenzie is always the center of attention."

"Basil, there's a difference between being the center of attention among strangers and getting attention from someone you really care about. You should give that some thought."

I had no idea what Gram was talking about. All I knew was that my birthday surprise for her had been a big flop, and it was all Tenzie's fault.

CHAPTER 7

The next day at lunch, I looked for Tenzie. I spotted her sitting with some kids I didn't know. They seemed to be talking with her, but I was too far away to hear the conversation. Since I didn't have to share the space, I could spread out my lunch the way I liked it.

Tenzie was talking, waving her hands around. I was distracted watching her, so I didn't see a couple of what looked like eighth-grade boys coming toward me. "We need that desk," the tall one said.

"But I haven't finished my lunch."

"So eat at a table like everybody else," the short kid said, as he and the other guy picked up my desk.

I tried to catch a hard-boiled egg as it slid to the floor. The short kid stepped on it, mashing the yolk into the floor. It wasn't an accident.

"Drop that desk right now." I looked up. It was Tenzie. She stood with her feet apart and her hands on her hips, like the gunslingers in the old cowboy movies Gram and I watched.

"Why should we?" the short guy challenged.

"Because Basil was using it, and I was just about to join him, that's why."

"We need this desk," tall guy said. "We have to stand on it to hang a banner."

Tenzie surprised both of them by giving the desk a yank that pulled it out of their hands. "You think this is the only desk in the building? There are empty desks all over the place. Go get one of them and leave us alone."

"Okay, sorry," tall guy said.

"And clean up this egg you smashed," Tenzie ordered, handing them a bunch of napkins. The two of them set to work, looking like puppies that had been scolded for peeing on the living room rug.

Tenzie grabbed a chair from the nearest table and sat down at my desk. "So what's up, Pesto?"

"Um, nothing much."

"I had fun at your grandmother's birthday party," she said. "Did you two play the game after I left?"

"No, it was too late to start." I didn't try to hide the fact that I was annoyed about that.

"I guess we spent too long with the stained glass. Sorry."

I couldn't think of anything to say, so I sat there chewing. I stole a look at Tenzie. I didn't know what to make of her. She didn't seem to be afraid of anybody. And if her feelings got hurt, it didn't last very long. I wished I could be more like her. I went around pretending nothing bothered me, but Tenzie really didn't care—about anything.

She looked up. "What's the matter?"

"Nothing."

"Why are you giving me the weird look?"

I shrugged. "I don't get you. Yesterday you went and sat at the eighth-grade girls' table, and today you tell off two eighth-grade boys. You can't go around doing things like that."

A crease formed between her eyebrows. "Why not?"

"Because people don't like it, that's why. You're supposed to hang out with kids your own age."

"Really. They have a rule here that says that?" She scrunched the paper all the way to the end of her straw.

"No, of course not. They don't need a rule because everybody just knows."

"Well, apparently not everybody." She blew the paper off her straw and hit my forehead dead center.

"What kind of a school did you go to before?" I asked. "Because I'm no expert, but I don't think this school is all that unusual."

"I've gone to a lot of schools. Every time my dad got fired as a weatherman, remember? Sometimes I barely got my name on the attendance list before we were packing up and moving on. So if you count the number of schools, I think I am an expert. I've been to at least ten of them. How many schools have you gone to?"

"Only this one," I said. "Unless I can count all those years being homeschooled by Gram."

"Your grandmother would be an awesome teacher," Tenzie said. "She knows about absolutely everything. Why isn't she still homeschooling you?"

"Gram knows everything except for little stuff like math and geography and science," I said. "So they wouldn't let her keep teaching me."

"Who's *they*?"

"I dunno. Whoever's in charge of homeschooled kids." That was a lie. Nobody told Gram she had to stop teaching me. And Gram didn't decide to stop because of her lack of math skills. It was me. I was the only home-schooled kid in the district, so I wanted to go to public school and meet other kids—to make friends. That was before I realized that in the real world, it was every kid for himself, and friends only messed up your life.

"Getting back to your rules," Tenzie said, "what was the problem with me yelling at those boys for trying to take the desk? They stopped, didn't they?"

"Yeah, but they were eighth-graders. You could've gotten us both killed."

Tenzie snitched an olive from my lunch and popped it into her mouth. "Oh, really. Who do you know that was killed by an eighth-grader?"

I didn't think that question deserved an answer. I guess Tenzie didn't either, because she went on. "I don't get why we have to stick with kids in our own grade. At my last school—well, actually the one before last—a couple of my best friends were in high school."

"No way," I said. "Why would high school kids want to hang around with you?"

"It was a school of the arts. We were all in shows together."

"You mean acting on a stage?" I asked.

"Yep. Singing and dancing, too. But I'm better at acting."

It was hard to picture scrawny little Tenzie performing in a show with high school kids. But it helped explain why she had so much nerve. If I ever had to get up on a stage, my heart would stop, no question about it. Big headlines—"It's Curtains for Kid Who Drops Dead in Middle of Play."

"I'll tell you the best thing about that school," Tenzie said. "Every kid there was creative in some way, and nobody worried about what other people thought. I had felt out of place in every school I went to before. But at SOTA, I wasn't the strangest kid in the school. I wasn't even close!" She leaned forward. "There was even a boy who had sort of the same thing with numbers and colors as me."

Frankly, I had started to zone out, which I often did when Tenzie was talking. But that woke me up. At first I thought I hadn't heard her right. "What about numbers and colors?"

The bell rang, and Tenzie gathered up her stuff.

"Never mind. I couldn't explain it to you if I tried. See you later, Pesto."

I ran over to dump my garbage in the can and took off after her. "Wait! Tell me what you mean!" But the hall was filled with kids, and I couldn't catch up with her.

All of a sudden, the short eighth-grade desk stealer was blocking my way. He put one hand against my chest, and I couldn't move. "You think you're a big shot, huh?"

"Who, me? No!"

He gathered up half of the material in my T-shirt and twisted it so it was almost choking me. "Next time I say I want your desk, you give it to me, understand?"

"Sure," I croaked.

As he let go of my shirt, he gave me a shove that knocked me to the floor. I was still picking up my stuff when the bell rang. I tried to slide into math class without being spotted by eagle-eyed Mrs. Lowe, but it didn't work.

She came over to my desk with a piece of paper. "I'm glad you decided to grace us with your presence, Basil. We're having a quiz today, so settle right in and get started."

I looked down at the math quiz and was immediately lost in the confetti design of colors. Tenzie was already hard at work. Then I noticed she was doing some kind of hand gestures. Was she sending me the solutions to the problems? The fingers on her right hand moved up as though they were climbing a ladder. Then she stopped and moved her fingers in a horizontal line to the right before putting down her answer.

"I don't get it," I whispered.

"Basil," Mrs. Lowe said. "Do you have a question?"

"No, ma'am."

"Then keep your eyes on your own paper."

I skipped the number problems at the top and moved down to the word problems, where the colors didn't jump out at me so much.

Max gave Susan ½ of his jelly beans. Right away I saw a white jelly bean and a blue one. You had to watch out for the white ones, because sometimes they were vanilla, which was delicious, but sometimes they were a really bad taste I couldn't even identify. Okay, wait, back to the problem. *Susan ate ½ of the jelly beans and gave the rest to Jason.* I ignored the blue and white thing here and focused on the problem. *Jason kept 8 of the jelly beans and gave the rest to Kara.* The number eight screamed purple. Purple jelly beans are my favorites. I wouldn't have given any of them to Kara.

How many jelly beans did Susan eat? That was a stupid question. How could you possibly know how many Susan ate? She might have put some away for later. Or maybe she didn't even like jelly beans and threw them away. In the space for the answer, I wrote, "There is no way to know this."

There were three other word problems, and they were just as confusing. One showed a staircase of three steps built with six cubes and wanted to know how many cubes it would take to make eleven steps. I must have stared at that picture for ten minutes before I started drawing cubes to figure it out. But by the time I got to eight steps, it was too big to fit on the paper. That's when Mrs. Lowe said, "Time's up, class. Please pass your papers to the front."

I had failed another math quiz, but it didn't matter. I had forgotten to put my name on my paper.

✛ ✛ ✛

I was waiting for Tenzie in my usual front seat on the bus, but before I could stop her, she went past me and sat somewhere in the back. Ever since I'd said I was trying to avoid her, she had stayed away from me. Not always, though. She came when I invited her to Gram's party, and she showed up when those guys were trying to steal my desk. It was hard to tell if she was mad at me or not.

Today I really wanted to talk with Tenzie. I needed to know what she meant by her numbers and colors thing. Was it possible she and I had the same thing, or did I just hear her wrong?

Then I waited for Tenzie. "You want to come over?" I asked. I wasn't going to blurt out my question right here in front of everybody.

"Okay, I don't have anything to do but homework," she said. "I can do that later. I'll wait until the bus leaves, though."

Mrs. Kenyon had a rule that she had to watch you cross to your own side of the road before she drove off. What she didn't know was that lots of kids crossed back to check their mailboxes as soon as she left. I crossed, and Tenzie followed soon after. When we got inside, I sat at the kitchen table right away to lead Tenzie away from my room. I didn't want her looking through my stuff again. There was a note from Gram on the table saying she'd be home soon. There was also a bowl of pistachio nuts. We talked about nothing while we cracked open the nuts, and I tried to find an opening for my question. Finally I just blurted it out. "What were you saying at lunch about numbers and colors?"

Tenzie shrugged. "It's nothing."

"No, really. I'm interested."

She looked up. "Why? Are you going to make fun of me?"

"Of course not. I have a thing with numbers and colors, too." There, I said it.

Her eyes narrowed. "What do you mean?"

I took a deep breath and jumped in with both feet. "When I see numbers, they have colors for me. I mean, I know they're really just black numbers on a white page, but in my mind, a four is pink, a five is orange— that kind of thing. And it works the other way around, too. Certain bright colors make me think of a number."

Tenzie didn't look shocked. "How do you make it happen?"

"I don't do anything. It's always been there. It messes me up in math."

"I see colors as numbers, too," Tenzie said, "but it makes math easier for me."

"Really? Does this have anything to do with those

hand signals you were trying to give me today in math class?"

"Those weren't signals. I was just following my grid."

"What's your grid?"

Tenzie stood up and closed her eyes for a few seconds. Then, when she opened them, she used her hands like a mime does when he's pretending he's inside a box. "The grid surrounds me on three sides. The single digits are along the bottom—that's blue. Then the next level up is blue-green—that's the tens." Tenzie's right index finger was tracing horizontal lines. "The third level is twenties—a bright green." She stopped and looked at me. "Can you see it?"

"I can sort of picture it in my head," I said.

"But you can't actually see it, going all the way up to here, with the hundreds at the top?" Her hand was raised way above her head now.

"No, sorry."

She came back to the table and slumped into a chair. "The only other person I've told about this is the kid from SOTA who saw numbers as colors, but he couldn't see my grid, either. He thought I was crazy." She looked hard at me. "You think I'm weird." It wasn't a question—just a statement of fact.

"Well, sure," I said. "I hate to be the one to break this to you, Tenzie, but we're both weird. Compared to most kids, we're off the charts."

She grinned at me. "We're interesting, though. Some kids are just weird and boring."

I liked that. Nobody had called me interesting before. "But I still don't get how you made your grid pop up. It's not there all the time, is it?"

"No. I make it happen by thinking about numbers. Once it's there, I can trace the levels, then move across the lines to find the numbers I need to solve math problems."

"So you figured out this system to make math easier?"

Even though there was nobody else around, she spoke just above a whisper. "It's almost like magic, Pesto. And it's not just for math. Sometimes when I'm scared about performing on stage, I think of numbers and bring up my grid. I put it between me and the audience. The bigger the numbers, the higher the grid wall. It glows with color, and it makes me feel safe."

"Whoa! You mean it's like a force field? Invisible to anybody but you?"

"Maybe it's a little like that. Wait . . . I have another

way to describe it. You know how the light shines through all the colored glass in your grandmother's hippie room? If you arranged all those pieces of glass by color in horizontal and vertical lines, you'd have my grid. That's the closest thing I've ever seen to it in real life."

Tenzie was waiting for me to show some sign that I understood what she was talking about. And in a way, I did, because the hippie room always set off so many numbers spinning in my head, I could hardly think.

"I'll show you. Do you have some crayons?"

"Sure. Hang on." I went into my room and grabbed my big tin box of markers. "How about these?"

Tenzie took the box from me. "Even better."

I gave her a couple pieces of art paper, and she picked through the markers to find the colors she needed. She made little squares of blue across three sides of a box. "It's ten across the front, then five on each side, so it wraps around me." Tenzie tried several markers on a piece of scrap paper before she came up with the right color for the second row.

"Green is next, right?" I handed her a green marker.

"Yes, but not that one." She fingered through the greens to find the perfect shade. I understood why it was so important to her to get the colors exactly right because I was the same way with the colors for my numbers. I could look at green things all day, but it was only a certain shade of green that triggered seven for me.

For the next half hour, I watched as Tenzie drew her magic grid, row by row. "There," she said, as she finished the top line of purple.

I held it up. "It's beautiful. The colors are in the same order as the rainbow."

She smiled. "I know, except mine starts with blue instead of red. That isn't anything I planned. It's always been that way. But I arrange everything like that in real life—crayons, sweaters in my closet."

That made me laugh. "I do the same thing. Those bottles of colored water in front of my window? I added food coloring a drop at a time to make them shade from each color to the next. I had them all arranged the way they would be in the rainbow."

"I should have noticed that," Tenzie said. "That's why it bugged you when I put the bottle back in the wrong place." She switched to the clean sheet of paper. "Here, write out your numbers for me using the right colors."

I found a thin black marker. "One is white, so I'll do it with a black outline."

Tenzie made a one below mine in blue. Then I took her blue and used it for my two. As we moved across the row, it was clear that we didn't have a single number/color combination in common.

When I wrote six in yellow, Tenzie had a fit. "You already used yellow for three."

"I know. They're both yellow. I get threes and sixes mixed up all the time."

"No wonder you have so much trouble in math."

"It gets worse," I said. "One and zero are both white."

We argued and laughed over whether seven was red or green and if nine was purple or brown. It felt great to share my freakism with somebody and not be teased about it.

I tried to imagine what it would be like to have all those lines of glowing colors pop up whenever I thought of numbers. Compared to what Tenzie had with her magic grid, I was practically normal and pretty close to being boring. But I sure wanted to know more about Tenzie Verplank.

CHAPTER

8

I could have gone on forever comparing my colors and numbers with Tenzie's, but we were interrupted by the ring of her cell phone. She didn't get to say anything after "Hi, Mom." She just kept nodding, as if her mother could see her through the phone. Finally she hung up without a good-bye. "I have to go home, Pesto. Mom wants to take me out to buy school supplies."

"Don't people usually do that before the first day of school?" I asked.

Tenzie shrugged. "My stuff isn't the highest priority in our family. First there's whatever Mom needs for work. Every time we move it's because Dad has to find a new job, so Mom has to take anything she can get. Next in line is Dad. He always gets some new weather-related tie for good luck. In his last job, he got a tornado tie. Do you have tornados here?"

"Not that I've ever seen," I said. "Mostly just snow."

"Dad's going to need a snowflake tie, then. I don't think he's ever had one. After that, it's my turn." Tenzie stopped at the door and turned. "Of course, that's only if Duncan doesn't need anything. He comes before me."

"Who's Duncan?" I asked. "Your brother?"

"Duncan is Mom's stupid canary," Tenzie said. "I do come before Bubbles, our goldfish, though. But I don't care because I hate shopping anyway. See you tomorrow, Pesto."

After the door closed, I sat there for a few minutes thinking about our conversation. I was so mad about how Tenzie got treated, it almost made me forget about the most amazing thing—that I wasn't the only person in the world who saw numbers as colors. Now I knew that, counting the kid at Tenzie's old school, there were at least three of us. And if there were three that we knew about, why couldn't there be more—maybe a lot more?

I went to my computer and did a search on *colors and numbers*. My computer took a little while to come up with two hundred and sixty-five million hits! I got all excited, but when I started clicking on the pages, I could tell they had nothing to do with what I was looking for.

I did another search—this time *seeing numbers as colors*. There were still tons of hits, but it didn't take long to find posts from people who described exactly what I had. There even was a message board where people were listing the colors for their numbers. They were all different and were arguing about whether a seven was blue or red. This made me laugh out loud because my seven is green. But even though the colors weren't the same, these were people just like me. And most of their posts sounded pretty intelligent. Then I looked at the top of the page and found the name for what we all had—synesthesia.

Now with a name, I could do a search on it. I came up with a bunch of hits, but as I clicked on the pages, I was disappointed to see most of them were written in scientific language, which was hard to understand. I got the general idea of it, though. In people with synesthesia, the nerves that carried the five senses to the brain got mixed up with each other. It wasn't just about numbers and colors. There were people who could taste sounds or smell textures.

I couldn't wait to tell Tenzie what I had discovered—that we had something unusual and special. It would be fun to look up more about it and to try to find somebody else who had Tenzie's magic grid.

I looked at the clock. Could she be back from shopping yet? I called her house, but there was no answer. I decided to go over there anyway and wait on her fake front porch.

Gram still wasn't home. I left a note before heading over to Tenzie's house. It always gave me the creeps to walk through Elegant Acres. As usual, there were no humans outdoors. The only living things were dogs, which would come charging out of their backyards, then slam on the brakes before they hit the boundaries of their underground electric fences. By the time I reached the turn to Tenzie's street, I had set off four dogs, who continued to bark at the edge of their yards, each in a slightly different pitch and rhythm.

There was no car in Tenzie's driveway, so I figured she was still out. Although that was hard to tell, because I noticed as people drove home, they pulled up to their mailboxes, then hit the automatic garage door openers and drove right in, as if they were being swallowed up by their identical houses.

I settled in on Tenzie's fake porch and watched a few more houses swallow cars. Then a car turned into Tenzie's driveway. It wasn't Tenzie and her mother, though. A tall, skinny guy parked in the driveway and walked toward the porch. He was wearing a blue tie with fluffy pink clouds on it, which gave me the clue that he was Tenzie's dad.

"Hello, are you selling something?"

I could only blurt out "No" before he went on.

"Oh, you're the paperboy, right? Do we get the paper? Is there a paper here?"

"I'm just waiting for Tenzie," I said. "She and her mother went shopping, but I think they'll be home soon."

"Oh," Mr. Verplank said. "Do you want to come in to wait?"

"No thanks. I'm fine here."

"Suit yourself." He shaded his eyes to look at the sky. "Feels like rain, don't you think?"

"Not really," I said. The only clouds in sight were on his tie.

Mr. Verplank squinted at me and nodded. "It's coming, though. I can feel it. The rain, that is." He got back in his car and pointed his remote at the garage door. It opened up and swallowed him. This time I had a strong feeling he was wrong about the rain.

It wasn't long before Tenzie and her mother came home and up the driveway. The garage gulped them in before I could call out to Tenzie. I couldn't tell if she'd seen me.

I was standing there, trying to decide whether or not to ring the doorbell, when Tenzie opened the door. "What are you doing here, Pesto?"

"I looked up what we have on the computer."

Tenzie gave me a puzzled look.

"You know," I said. "The numbers and colors thing. We're not the only ones. It's pretty rare, but I found a message board with a lot of people who have it."

Tenzie looked interested. "How do you know they have the same thing as us?"

"I'll show you. Do you have a computer?"

"Yes, but my father's home now, so he's using it for his weather stuff."

"Well, can you come over to my house? I book-marked the best sites."

Tenzie called back into the house. "I'm going out for a while. I'll be back for dinner." Nobody answered.

She bounded off the fake porch ahead of me.

I ran to catch up with her. "It has a name. It's called syn-es-thesia."

Tenzie laughed. "It's sinful?"

"No, it's spelled *S-Y-N* not *S-I-N*. It means the wires of your senses get crossed. And it's not just numbers and colors. Some people can taste textures. One guy said whenever he heard a truck drive by his house, he smelled bacon."

"Can you imagine?" Tenzie said. "He must be hungry all the time."

"This is the best part." I had to run a few steps to keep up with her. "People in the arts are seven times more likely to have synesthesia than anybody else. How cool is that?"

"Does that count people who like to act?" Tenzie asked.

"I think so. People who act, sing, write, play music, paint—they're all artsy."

We arrived at my house and headed straight for my computer, passing Gram in the kitchen. "Hi, kids. What's going on?"

"We're doing some research for a science project, Gram. We need one of the kitchen chairs so we can both sit at the computer."

For some reason, Gram seemed to believe me and didn't ask any more questions. Even now that I knew lots of people had synesthesia, I wasn't ready to tell her about it. I turned on the computer and went to the first site I had bookmarked.

Tenzie started scrolling through the information. "A lot of people seem to see numbers as colors, but I don't see anything like my magic grid."

"I didn't find that yet," I said, "but some people see the months of the year spread out around them. Do you have that?"

She shook her head. "No, but the days of the week have colors for me. Oh, look. It says here that people with synesthesia tend to be psychic. I'm pretty sure I am. What about you?"

"I don't think so," I said. "What makes you think you're psychic?"

"I've had a few dreams that something bad would happen, and in the next few days, it comes true. Or sometimes I'm thinking about somebody, and the phone rings and it's them. Or maybe I can tell what somebody is thinking before they say it. Stuff like that. If you really pay attention, I bet you'll find you're psychic, too."

I didn't say anything, but just nodded. I liked knowing that I wasn't alone with the synesthesia, but I wasn't sure I wanted to know ahead of time that bad things were going to happen.

Tenzie grinned. "It's not scary, Basil."

Had she just read my mind? I couldn't tell.

Tenzie jumped up from the computer. "I have a great idea. Let's ask around school to see if other kids have this. Maybe we could start a club or something and learn more about it."

Tenzie sure wasn't reading my mind now. "No way! Letting people know about my numbers and colors secret opened me up to a lot of teasing. I don't want to start that all over again."

"I've always kept quiet about it, too," she said, "but now that I know how special it is, I want to tell every-body." Then maybe she read my mind or at least read the expression on my face. "But if that's the way you want it, Pesto, it can be our secret."

+ + +

After dinner that night, Gram pulled a letter out of her pocket and handed it to me. As soon as I touched it, I had a funny feeling that it was bad news. "What's this?"

"It's from your mother, Basil."

"Carly?" We hadn't heard much from her in the past few years, except for sending cards on our birthdays—well, some of our birthdays. "I don't want to read it. Just tell me what she said."

"She's coming home."

I couldn't believe it. I had given up on my mother sending for me to go to Hollywood, but the thought of her coming home had never crossed my mind. She didn't even seem like a real person to me. "You mean she's coming back to live here?"

"She doesn't say. All I know is, she got on a bus two days ago, and she'll be here early tomorrow morning."

I couldn't decide if this was a good thing or not. But if Tenzie was right about me being psychic, I wasn't looking forward to what would happen when my mother arrived.

CHAPTER

9

We were in Gram's truck with no breakfast, heading into Broxburg before the sun came up. That was the closest the bus line came to our little town. My stomach was rolling over, but I wasn't sure whether it was from hunger or the prospect of seeing my mother for the first time in seven years. "I don't feel so good," I said.

Gram glanced at her watch. "If I take you back home, I'll have to drop you off and run. We're barely going to get there in time for the bus, Basil. You took too long to get moving this morning."

"Yeah, I know. Sorry." What Gram didn't know was that I hardly slept all night. I had a nightmare that when my mother got off the bus, she looked exactly like the green witch in the Oz movie. Then when I tried to run away from her, she sent her creepy flying monkeys after me. They kept dive-bombing me so I had to swat them away. When I woke up, I discovered that I had knocked all my paperback books off the shelf over my head. It took me a long time to get back to sleep afterward. The only comfort was knowing that meeting my mother this morning couldn't be half as bad as the dream. At least there wouldn't be any flying monkeys.

Bumping along in the truck, I ran my tongue over my furry teeth. I should have brushed, or used mouthwash in case I was expected to hug her or kiss her or something. What *was* I supposed to do? Was my mother still my mother, even if she didn't raise me? This person I was going to meet at the bus station was a stranger. I didn't owe her anything. But the biggest question in my mind was why she had decided to come home.

"Don't you think Carly is just coming for a visit, Gram? I mean she's not going to stay here, is she? After living out in Hollywood, she'd be bored silly in Hayes Corners."

"I'll be surprised if she stays here for more than a week, Basil. California is a pretty magnetic place. Your grandfather and I often talked about going back to San Francisco someday. It probably wouldn't have lived up to my romanticized memories of it, though."

I was used to life with just Gram and me. Even the remote possibility that Carly was moving home made my stomach start to heave big-time. I tried to hold it back, but it didn't work. "I'm going to be sick," I croaked.

Gram looked at me. "You want me to stop right here?"

I clamped my mouth shut, nodded, and slapped on the window. Gram swerved onto the shoulder, and I jumped out before she came to a full stop, spewing vomit as soon as I hit the ground. Gram came around the car and held my head until I was finished, the same way she had done since I was a little kid. That's what a real mother did. "Are you all right?" she asked, after my retching stopped.

I wiped my mouth on the back of my hand. "Yeah, I guess so." We climbed back into the truck and started off down the road. I kept my eyes on the farthest point the headlights lit up to keep from getting queasy again.

Gram fumbled in her purse without looking away from the road. "Here, chew up a couple of these." A roll of Life Savers hit my palm.

I popped one in my mouth. Wintergreen. I had

always hated that flavor, but at least it was strong enough to cover up the taste of puke.

"Are you sick because you're nervous about seeing Carly again?" Gram asked.

I noticed that she didn't refer to her as my mother.

"No," I said. "She's nobody to me, so why should I care?"

"I know how you feel, Basil, but it will be easier if we both try to make the best of this. Carly was always headstrong, even as a little girl. It can't be easy for her to come home without accomplishing what she set out to do."

"She's been gone for seven years," I said. "How long does it take to figure out you're not going to be a big-deal movie star?"

"She didn't choose an easy life for herself," Gram said. "Thousands of young girls go out to Hollywood thinking they'll become famous, and most of them leave bitter and disappointed."

"Oh, this is going to be great, having a bitter and disappointed bad actress living with us," I said. "I can hardly wait."

Gram nudged me with her elbow. "Chill out, Basil. You're making this harder on yourself. Before you know it, Carly will have flown the coop, and we'll be back to normal."

We rode along in silence after that, giving me plenty of time to stew over the fact that my mother walked out on me when I was five years old and had barely tried to contact me since. And now Gram wanted me to be nice to her? I was supposed to feel sorry that she didn't turn out to be a famous star? Yeah, right.

I could see buildings in the distance and figured we must be getting near Broxburg.

"Keep your eyes open for Harvey's Diner, Basil. The bus station is in the building right next to it." Gram reached over and squeezed my hand. That was her way of saying she knew how I felt, and everything would be okay. Gram and I didn't always have to say things to understand each other.

"There it is!" I said, pointing to the flickering neon sign of a big yellow coffee cup with pink squiggly steam lines rising up from it. Gram pulled into the parking lot, and we went to sit on a bench outside the diner under the bus stop sign. Gram looked over and smiled at me. She was twisting the strap of her purse—a dead giveaway that she was as worried as me about what was going to get off that bus. The neon sign sputtered, making the hairs rise on the back of my neck.

I heard a deep roar, then a huge silver bus lumbered around the corner and headed for us. It rocked from side to side a few times on the potholed street and stopped just beyond us, letting out a whoosh of air from its brakes.

I could make out the shapes of people getting up from their seats. Gram walked over to the bus door, but I stayed where I was. I wanted to see Carly before I had to talk with her—size her up. I knew from pictures that she was pretty, with long dark brown hair, so that's what I was watching for.

The door opened, and the driver got off first, going over to open the long compartment under the bus where they kept the suitcases. Everybody seemed to be leaving the bus and going into the diner for breakfast. I took inventory as they filed past me—old skinny guy, old fat guy, soldier coming home on leave, mother with two kids. Gram was watching them, too. Then she sort of backed off. Had Carly missed the bus? I was surprised to feel a little bit disappointed. Nobody else was getting off, then the driver reached up to help somebody down the steps. I leaned forward to see. It was just a little old lady. She must have been clogging up the aisle, because there were people behind her. One was a thin girl with short bleached blond hair. I figured she was with the old lady because she had been carrying the woman's purse and handed it to her when they were both on the sidewalk. I strained to see who else was getting off.

Suddenly, Gram walked over to the blond girl. She didn't hug her or anything, but they were talking to each other. Gram turned and pointed at me. Was that Carly? The girl smiled and waved, then started running toward me with her arms outstretched. I scrunched down on the bench, but there was nothing to hide behind. Judging by the bolt of fear that shot through me, she might as well have been the green witch. She pulled me up off the bench and nearly hugged the breath out of me. Her perfume was the same as I remembered, and for a second, I zinged back to that five-year-old kid sitting on her lap in the picture. Then she grabbed me by the shoulders and held me at arm's length.

"Hi, Basil."

"Hi, um . . . hi." I almost called her Mommy. That would have been humiliating.

I started to pull away, but Carly tightened her grip.

"Wait. Let me look at you a minute. You've grown so much."

Grown? What did she expect—that I'd stay in a little cocoon until she decided to come see me? I ducked my head, not wanting to look her in the eyes. Gram saved me. "Carly, let's get your bags into the car, then we can have some breakfast in the diner. You must be hungry." Gram turned to me. "If that's okay with you, Basil. Are you feeling better now?"

Carly looked worried. "Are you sick, baby?"

"No, I'm fine." I got away from her this time.

"Okay, let's get the bags," Carly said. "The driver is pulling them out right now—those two purple ones."

Gram and Carly got the suitcases and locked them in the truck. I stood there as if my feet were part of the sidewalk. Next thing I knew, I was being steered into the diner. Gram slid into a booth, and I dove in beside her. As soon as we were all seated, I realized my mistake. I hadn't wanted to sit close to my mother, but now I found myself face-to-face with her, unable to avoid her teary-eyed gaze.

The waitress came with water and menus, and that took Carly's attention off me for a minute, so I could study her. It was the same face in the picture at home, still pretty, but thinner, and cartoon-painted. Her hair was like straw—stiff and straight—sticking out from her head in uneven hunks. A couple of tiny barrettes with sparkly purple stones held one chunk of hair out of her eyes. I could see dark roots—probably her real color. Her eyelashes were all spiky black with purple smudged on her eyelids and under her eyes. The makeup must have smeared from sleeping on the bus, because nobody would look like that on purpose.

Carly glanced up and caught me looking at her. I chugged half a glass of water and concentrated on the menu. Whenever we used to come into Broxburg, I always got the banana chocolate-chip pancakes. That was before Gram and I stopped eating wheat, and they didn't even sound good to me anymore.

I kept my eyes on the menu to avoid joining the conversation. Well, actually there wasn't any conversation to join. When the waitress came back to the table, Gram ordered scrambled eggs and bacon. Then Carly said, "I have to have those banana chocolate-chip pancakes. They were always my favorites."

The waitress was staring at me now, waiting for me to say something. I blurted out the first thing I saw on the menu. "I'll have a bowl of oatmeal."

Gram looked up, surprised—she knew I hated oatmeal—but she didn't say anything. I decided oatmeal was a perfect choice for this meal—a big gray tasteless blob in a bowl. If I was going to be miserable, I might as well go all the way.

After the waitress gathered up our menus, Carly caught my eye again. "You must think I'm a terrible mother."

Wow, I didn't expect her to say that. I didn't know how to answer.

She smiled at me and winked. "You didn't think I'd forget to bring you a present, did you?" She dug through the huge shoulder bag she'd been carrying and fished out a small stuffed dog. "You were always teasing to get a dog. Did you ever get one?" She bounced it across the table toward me, then shook it so its ears flapped.

"Yeah, but he died," I mumbled, wondering why she thought a stupid stuffed dog would make her eligible for the mother of the year award.

Gram nailed me in the ankle with the toe of her shoe.

I grabbed the dog and set it on the table. "Thanks. It's—um—cute."

Carly smiled. "That was just a little joke. I knew you were too old for stuffed animals, so I got this for you, too." She pawed through the bag again and held out the portable version of the Vampire Smasher video game. Even though I loved board games, this was the one video game I'd been dying to get and was planning to put it on my Christmas list. It was expensive, so it was the only thing I was going to ask for. But I didn't want it this way—not from a mother who was trying to buy off seven years of guilt.

Carly put the game box on the table. "I didn't know what you'd like. I don't ever see any kids, you know? Maybe I got the wrong thing." She bit her bottom lip.

"No, it's okay," I said.

Gram wasn't being any help at all. She was pretending to study the menu, but our bench was shaking from the constant tapping of her foot. I couldn't remember ever seeing Gram like this. She was usually so laid back.

"That's good then," Carly said. Her eyes still glittered with a few tears. "I'm glad that we're getting reacquainted, Basil."

This was worse than I could have imagined. I didn't know what to say, or what to do with my face, or how to get the heck out of there. I looked frantically around the diner. Where were those darn flying monkeys when you really needed them?

CHAPTER

10

Somehow, I got through breakfast with Gram and Carly. I even managed to eat the oatmeal, which was grayer and blobbier than any bowl of oatmeal I could remember. But I ate the whole thing because it fit the mood of the occasion perfectly. I also managed to refuse the bites of my favorite banana chocolate-chip pancakes that Carly kept offering me every other minute.

Even though the front seat of the truck was big enough for three people, I jammed myself into the space behind the seat, which wasn't really meant for a person older than about five.

"Oh, look," Carly said. "The bakery is open. Can we

stop for cookies? You always used to let me get those huge peanut butter ones when we came into town, Mom. I want to get some for Basil."

"We don't eat that junk anymore," Gram said. "Besides, we don't have the time. Basil will miss the school bus."

Carly looked over her shoulder at me. "Oh, Basil, it's my first day home. You can skip school today, and we can hang out together."

Gram and I spoke in unison.

"No, he can't."

"No, I can't."

Carly shrugged. "All right, if you both want to be party poopers."

On the way home, I didn't try to help Gram out with the awkward conversation she and Carly were having up front. Gram never asked the real question I wanted to hear the answer to. Was Carly staying for a few days or forever? I couldn't figure it out from Carly's luggage. She didn't need two suitcases for a couple of days, but no way she could have stuffed seven years of her belongings into them. So that whole big question dangled in the air above us like a cat who could climb trees but didn't know how to get down. You just knew that, sooner or later, that cat would let loose and land on your head. When Carly tried to catch my eye in the rearview mirror, I shoved over some boots and old jackets and skootched out of her range. Then, when she tried to turn around to say something to me, I squeezed directly behind her so she'd have to have the swivel neck of an owl to see me. Pretty soon she gave up, and the drone of the truck's engine made me drift off to sleep.

I didn't wake up until I heard the crunch of the tires on our gravel driveway. I had a couple seconds of trying to figure out what the heck had happened to my bedroom. Then it all came rushing back to me—the bus, the diner, Carly—and I knew where I was. As soon as we came to a stop, I jumped out and ran for the house. By the time they got Carly's suitcases out of the truck bed, I had my school stuff and was heading out the door again. I ducked away from Carly's hug. "Gotta go. Gonna miss the bus," I said.

Gram started to say something, then clamped her mouth shut and gave me a look. Hey, Carly didn't know that the bus stopped in front of our house and that it wasn't due for another twenty minutes. She wouldn't even know I was lying to get away from her.

I hid behind the big oak tree at the far edge of our property and watched as the Elegant Acres kids crossed and gathered at the end of our driveway. When the bus came, I waited until almost everybody was on before I ran for it. As we drove off, I thought I saw Carly's face in the kitchen window. I ducked.

My seat was empty. I scanned the bus and saw Tenzie about halfway back, but I couldn't catch her eye because she was busy talking to some kid I didn't know. I guess she had figured I was staying home, so she didn't sit in our usual seat. I didn't see her again until lunch. She came rushing across the cafeteria, looking as if her world had just fallen apart. "Pesto, did you hear the terrible news?"

I was pretty sure she wasn't talking about *my* terrible news. I hadn't said anything to anybody about Carly. Actually, Tenzie was the first person I had talked to all day, not counting saying "I don't know" to the science teacher's question about nimbus clouds, "I'm not sure" to the social studies teacher's question about what was the longest river in South America, and "thank you" to the cafeteria cashier when she gave me change for my milk.

"What terrible news?" I asked.

Tenzie sat down and dug into her lunch bag. "Remember I told you Mrs. Fischer was going to start a seventh-grade after-school drama club, and they were having auditions for *Peter Pan* this Friday?"

"Yeah, I guess." I had a vague memory of Tenzie talking about some play she wanted to be in. When Tenzie went on and on about something I didn't care about, I just tuned her out and kept saying "uh-huh," or maybe "wow!" if I could tell I was supposed to be excited about it.

"So, that's why the whole thing has fallen apart," Tenzie was saying.

"Uh-huh," I mumbled, wondering what I had missed while I was thinking about how I tune her out.

"Basil!"

I snapped to attention. "I mean, wow! What happened?"

She rolled her eyes. "I just told you, Mrs. Fischer is moving to Georgia because she got a job as a drama teacher at a college. Were you listening to me at all?"

"Yeah, sure I was listening. So why can't somebody else take Mrs. Fischer's place?"

"Because it's a huge job, that's why. And they need somebody who knows about theater. You can't just walk in off the street and direct a play, especially a musical. Mrs. Fischer was a drama major in college, you know."

I didn't know that, but I figured Mrs. Fischer couldn't have been all that good, or she'd be an actress instead of an English teacher. All of a sudden, my world was crawling with bad actresses, and I had a sneaking suspicion that Tenzie might be one, too.

"We would have had so much fun in that play, Pesto. I know you say you can't learn lines, but you would have been perfect for the part of the dog. All he says is 'woof!'"

Sheesh! The dog? I might not be great at memorizing things, but I certainly could handle something a little more complicated than "woof." That is if I wanted to, which I didn't.

"Yeah, well, I guess I missed my big chance at stardom," I said. "Now I'll never be famous."

The bell rang, and it was time to go to math. I had wanted to tell Tenzie about Carly, but for some reason I couldn't bring it up. I knew this was the kind of thing you were supposed to talk over with a friend. This was more important than a stupid drama club. This was my whole life turning into a drama.

I didn't bring it up when we were sitting together on the bus, mainly because we got to our stop and I could see Carly sitting on the front porch. I didn't feel up to facing her. I stopped Tenzie when she got off. "Hey, could I come over to your house for a while? I forgot that Gram had to go somewhere."

Tenzie glanced at our driveway. "Has she taken up hiking? Because her truck is right there." She squinted at me. "What's the matter? You sick or something?"

"No, forget it." I was going to have to go home sooner or later. Might as well get it over with.

"Basil! You're home!" Carly was waving frantically.

"Who's that?" Tenzie asked.

"Never saw her before," I said.

"I've been waiting all day to talk to my boy!" Carly called out.

"For a stranger, she seems to know *you* pretty well," Tenzie said.

"Yeah, well, I'll see you tomorrow."

As I turned to cross the street, Tenzie grabbed my arm. "Wait, she's your mother, isn't she?"

I shrugged. "Maybe."

Tenzie's fingers were digging into my arm. "The mother from Hollywood? The mother who's an *actress?*" Tenzie's voice had risen to a squeak, and she was definitely cutting off my circulation by the time she got to the end of that second sentence.

"Yeah, she's both of those mothers," I said, pulling away from her grip.

"I want to meet her."

"Maybe some other time," I said. "She's tired from her trip. Let's go to your house."

"She doesn't look tired to me." Carly was waving both arms now. Tenzie dragged me across the road without looking either way. Unfortunately no huge truck was coming, so we made it safely to the other side.

Tenzie bounded up onto the porch. "Hi, I'm Tenzie Verplank, Basil's best friend. I'm an actress, too."

Carly's face lit up like a Christmas tree. "I didn't know Basil had a best friend. That's simply fantastic! And it sounds as if Basil has told you about me."

I wanted to tell Carly that she didn't know anything about me and that all the information I had given Tenzie about her was one sentence. Two sentences, tops.

But they were both babbling, ignoring me. I was surprised that Carly looked as bad as she had when she got off the bus. She was wearing different clothes though, and had some little feather things in her hair instead of the sparkly barrettes. You'd think if she went to the trouble of doing that, she could have combed her hair and washed that junk off her face.

"I just love the way you wear your hair, Carly," Tenzie was saying.

My eyes shot over to Carly to see if she had caught the sarcasm.

She hadn't. "Thank you, Tenzie. I'm afraid I'll have a hard time getting someone around here to cut it this way."

"Maybe if you ask Gram, she'll run over your head with the lawnmower," I mumbled.

Neither one of them heard me. They were talking about makeup now. I looked more closely at Carly's face and saw brown eye smudges where the purple ones had been. She had washed off the mess and made a whole new one—on purpose! And the most confusing thing of all was that Tenzie thought she looked great.

Carly turned to me. "Sorry about the girl talk, Basil. I made a snack. Let's all sit down and have a little getting-to-know-you party." There was a huge plate of chocolate-chip cookies on the table.

"I'm so excited to meet you," Tenzie said. "I've always wanted to go to Hollywood. I mean, we lived in California once but never got there. My father's in the entertainment business, too."

I raised my eyebrows at her. I had seen Mr. Verplank's weather report, and *entertainment* wasn't a word I'd use to describe it. Well, he was usually pointing to a different town than he was talking about, which was kind of funny, but it wasn't on purpose, so it didn't count.

"Your father's an entertainer?" Carly looked interested. "What does he do?"

"He's in television," Tenzie said. "Not in this town, of course. He has to commute to the TV station in Broxburg."

"He's just the local weatherman," I said.

Tenzie shot me a look. "Well, you have to be an actor for that job, you know. You can't just stand there like a lump and read the forecast."

"That's very true," Carly said. "Making something dull like the weather sound interesting takes a lot of talent."

Tenzie gave me a smug smile, then turned to Carly. "So how long will you be staying here?"

The air seemed to vibrate with that question. Carly winked at me. "I was a bit uncertain, but I can't tear myself away from Basil. I don't have any plans to go back to California."

When Carly's words finally got through to me, the treed cat landed on my head with a thud. She was staying, and it was all my fault.

Tenzie and Carly talked about Hollywood and acting—things that didn't interest me at all. Neither one of them noticed when I left to go find Gram.

She was where I thought she'd be, cutting stained glass in the hippie room.

"How come you're not with Carly?" I asked.

The cutter made a crunching sound as Gram traced a long, curved line across a piece of deep purple-blue glass—the perfect color for eight. When she got to the end of the cut, Gram looked up. "Carly and I have to take each other in small doses. We've always been too much alike."

"Alike! You're nothing like Carly at all. A person can count on you. Carly just runs off and does whatever she wants, no matter who she hurts."

Gram tapped along the curved line with the ball end of the cutter, then took hold of the glass and pressed it down over the edge of the table. I loved to watch this part, where the split raced perfectly along the score, separating the pieces in two. "Give Carly the benefit of the doubt, Basil. I don't think I've ever told you how I ended up in San Francisco, did I?"

"No."

"I was never a good student in high school, but I loved drawing and painting. My art teacher felt that I was talented, so he helped get me into an art school in Philadelphia. My grades were awful. I'm sure he had to pull a few strings to do it. When I got there, the art courses turned out to be a lot harder than I had expected because I had to do assignments, rather than just painting what I felt like. And it was a long, miserable winter—cold and snowy. Then I saw on the news that college and high school students were flocking to Haight-Ashbury in San Francisco for spring break. They called themselves hippies and flower children. The girls wore flowers in their hair, and they were singing and dancing, and it was warm and sunny. It looked like heaven to me. I sold all my school books and my art supplies, and bought a bus ticket."

"You quit school?"

"I did. And if you ever do a thing like that, I'll wring

your neck. I'm only telling you this so you can understand where Carly gets her wanderlust. It's in her genes."

That was a hard picture to get into my head—Gram young and flighty and running away from responsibility just like Carly.

Gram was in the middle of making another curved cut. I usually didn't distract her when she was cutting, but I blurted out, "I think her wanderlust is over, Gram, because she says she's staying here for good."

"You can't always believe what Carly says. Just go with the flow. She'll be taking off any day now." Gram tapped along the cut line and pushed it against the table edge. But this time, the split ran off from the curve and fractured the piece of glass. Gram groaned as she dropped the smaller pieces into the scrap box under the table.

"Sorry I messed you up, Gram."

Gram moved a paper pattern around on the larger piece of glass until it fit, then traced around it with a black marker. "It's not your fault, Basil. I let myself lose focus."

I wanted to believe Gram, but Carly might have settled down since the old days. Still, Gram didn't seem worried about Carly hanging around, so I decided to take things one day at a time. As I was leaving the hip-pie room, I heard the soft crunch of the glass cutter, followed by the chink of shattering glass as a piece hit the floor.

Two cutting disasters in one day? I couldn't remember the last time Gram had broken glass.

CHAPTER
11

Carly and Tenzie barely noticed when I got back to the kitchen. Their heads were bent over a scrapbook of pictures from a play.

"That's you, right?" Tenzie said, pointing at a girl dressed like a waitress at the Hayes Corners Oktoberfest.

Carly nodded. "Yes, it is."

"You played Maria?" Tenzie squealed. "The lead in *Sound of Music*?"

Carly flipped the page. "That was my junior year. I played another Maria senior year."

"Maria in *West Side Story*!" Tenzie's voice rose another octave.

"Big deal," I said, slipping into a chair. "They were just high school plays. It's not like it was Hollywood or something."

Carly looked hurt for a second. I almost regretted what I had said, but she was filling the whole house like a balloon in the Macy's Thanksgiving Day Parade, and I just wanted to let some air out of her to make room for the rest of us.

"A high school play is a very big deal," Tenzie said. "I'd like to see you get a part in one."

Carly closed the scrapbook. "No, Basil is right. I nailed the lead every time I tried out in high school, and it gave me kind of a swelled head. I thought I was incredibly talented, until I arrived in Hollywood, where I was competing with the most gifted actors from every town in America. I went to hundreds of auditions, and all I ever got was a small part in one of those afternoon TV movies."

Tenzie's eyes grew wide. "You don't mean you were in an Afternoon Family Theater Production! Which one? I've seen all of those movies—practically know them by heart. Did it have animals? A dog, or a horse, or a flock of geese?"

Carly laughed. "No animals. It was the one

where . . . Well, Basil, you must have the DVD I sent you. Maybe Tenzie would like to see it."

I shrugged. "I don't remember any movie. And if there was a DVD, it probably got thrown out."

Carly's smile faded. "My mother never showed you my movie?"

"I guess not. Or if I saw it, I can't remember it."

Tenzie stuck an elbow in my ribs and glared at me. She didn't know I was lying. I had been so excited the day of Carly's movie, I kept turning on the TV every half hour to make sure it was working. When Carly finally came on the screen, my heart almost stopped beating. She played the part of a young mother, and every time she had a close-up, I was sure she was talking right to me, her kid. Gram recorded the show, and I played it over and over, backing it up so many times to watch Carly's scenes that I finally messed up the cable box and the movie was toast. It was like losing her all over again. Then Carly's DVD had arrived, and I played it so many times, I ruined that, too.

For the next couple of years after seeing that show, I had been convinced this was the beginning of Carly's movie career and she'd be sending for me any day.

I believed that for a long time. It took a few more years of letdowns to make me wise up.

Tenzie was still going with the questions. "Even if we can't see it, tell me about the movie. What was your character's name?"

"I've forgotten," Carly said. "Basil is right. It wasn't a very memorable movie."

Tenzie rested her chin on her fist and gazed at Carly with such admiration, I wanted to puke. "That doesn't matter, Carly. The point is, you were brave enough to move all the way across the country and go to those auditions. That's exactly what I want to do when I grow up."

Carly put her arm around Tenzie's shoulders and gave her a squeeze. "Give it a lot of thought before you do. Hollywood isn't as glamorous as it sounds."

I wanted to ask Carly if it took a lot of courage to run off and leave her little kid behind. I had been old enough to know she was dumping me, and I could still remember crying for months, with Gram telling me over and over to be a big, brave boy and everything would be all right. Well, it wasn't all right then. And it wasn't all right now.

My life completely changed that week. Gram had always let me have my own space, but Carly was on me like a fly on dog poop the second I got home from school every day, and I couldn't shoo her away. I tried to use homework as an excuse to be alone in my room, but she was constantly barging in and offering to help me study. Now school was the place I went to for peace and solitude.

The following Tuesday, Tenzie came into lunch with the look that usually meant she was cooking up some kind of plan.

"What's going on?" I asked.

"Tryouts after school today. You didn't forget, did you?"

"I thought you said Mrs. Fischer couldn't direct the play."

Tenzie raised her eyebrows. "I hear she got someone to take her place."

"That's nice, but I told you I'm not interested."

She pulled up a chair. "You have to come, even if you're not going to audition."

"Why?"

"Because I need you there to keep me from getting

nervous." She looked at me with the kind of big, sad eyes that make people take stray puppies home with them. "Please, Basil."

Even though Tenzie seemed full of confidence, she had told me how being onstage terrified her. I couldn't understand why she made herself audition when she got so scared, but the least I could do was support her.

"Okay, I'll go with you."

Tenzie's face lit up. "Thanks, Basil. Meet me at the back of the auditorium after school." She started down the hall to her next class.

"Wait," I called. "Will you be done in time for the late bus?"

"We don't need the bus," Tenzie yelled over her shoulder. "We have a ride." I wondered who would be giving us a ride. Maybe her mother or father? Then I went on to woodworking class and forgot about it.

Woodworking was my best subject because I'd been building stuff with Gram for as long as I could remember. While other kids were doing simple projects like bluebird houses and boards for hanging keys, I was making a small cabinet to hold Gram's board games. At the beginning of the year, when I had brought in the directions from Gram's *Furniture*

Builder magazine, my teacher, Mr. Clemens, had told me it was too difficult, but he finally decided I knew what I was doing and offered me some tips to make it even better.

There was a drawer at the top for card games, and the bottom had three shelves for board games. Mr. Clemens suggested that I add a door with a latch. It was a good idea and made it look really nice. I had tried to have it done in time for Gram's birthday, but I didn't make my deadline. I didn't tell her about the cabinet then, though. I wanted to see the surprise on her face when I brought it home.

I finished the fine sanding during class. Then all that was left to do was staining it and putting the latch on the door. I was glad I'd saved the surprise. Gram hadn't been herself since Carly came home, so I thought maybe this would cheer her up.

When I got to the auditorium after class, Tenzie was just inside the door. "I was beginning to think you forgot. Follow me. I have a surprise for you."

"I don't like surprises," I said, trying to hang back.

"Oh, come on." Tenzie grabbed me by the elbow and pulled me down the aisle. The kids were gathered around Mrs. Fischer and some other person I couldn't see. Tenzie ran over to the group while I looked for a seat away from the action so I could be invisible.

Mrs. Fischer clapped her hands. "Everybody sit down." Kids quickly filled in all the seats except the ones near me. "As you know, I've had to give up directing our show. I'm sorry to leave, but delighted to turn over the reins to someone with real experience in the field of entertainment. It's a pleasure to introduce your new drama club director."

I turned to look at the clock at the back of the auditorium, wondering how soon I could get out of there, when Mrs. Fischer said, "This is Charlize LeMay, a real Hollywood actress."

I didn't recognize the name, but I whipped my head around at the words *Hollywood actress*. I was pretty sure that Hayes Corners wouldn't have more than one of them at a time. Then a kid moved out of the way, and I saw the messy hair and sparkly hair clips. It was Carly, with Tenzie standing right next to her. As if that weren't bad enough, Tenzie announced, "Guess who Charlize LeMay is? She's Basil's mother."

All eyes turned to me. It was as if a huge spaceship hovered over me, pouring a blinding beam of light on my head. So much for being invisible.

Joel Mack plopped himself into the seat next to me. "You trying out, Basil?" he asked.

It was weird to hear my name come out of his mouth. "Me? No."

Joel slumped down in his seat. "Well, I have to. My girlfriend wants me to be Captain Hook. She's going to be Peter Pan."

His girlfriend? I followed his gaze and saw Ashleigh Gianelli giving him a smile and one of those subtle little finger waves.

"Isn't Peter Pan a guy's part?" I asked.

Joel turned his attention back to me. "That's what I thought, but Ashleigh says Peter Pan is always played by a girl. So can you get your mother to give me the Captain Hook part?"

"I don't know. I guess you'll get the part if you're good enough."

Joel put his hand to the side of his mouth and whispered. "Look, I'm a football player, not an actor, okay? So I'm not getting the part unless you make it happen."

"But . . . but I—"

"Yeah, yeah," Joel interrupted. "You want to know what's in it for you, right? Well, there's this weekend football league that I started. It's not official, no parents or anything. It's mostly seventh-graders from our school and Saint Catherine's. Anyway, I'm in charge of the whole thing. If you convince your mother to give me the part, you can be on my team. Deal?"

First of all, the thought of playing football made my teeth curl. Especially a game where big jocks like Joel would get to beat on me with no adult around to blow a whistle to call them off. I tried not to let the fear show on my face. I just said, "Okay. Deal."

Joel went back over to Ashleigh and whispered something in her ear. Ashleigh smiled and sent a finger wave my way. This time I blushed. That girl was unbelievably gorgeous.

Carly was standing in the middle of the stage under one of the overhead lights. She had on a black top and pants and tall black boots with high heels. Over that she had some kind of loose silver sweater that sparkled like diamonds. I had to admit, except for the messy hairstyle and makeup, she looked like a star.

"Okay, everybody," Carly said. "Let's get started. I hope you've been thinking about what part you want to audition for. Come up to the table and get a script page for your character. Then you'll have about ten minutes to go over it before we start. I'm going to audition all of the Wendys first." Carly went to the side of the stage and sat cross-legged on a long table. I was having a hard time getting used to the fact that I was looking at the mother I had wondered about all those years. Carly didn't even come close to the image I'd had in my head.

The first to audition was a girl named Amy. She was so scared, she could hardly say her name. "Don't be nervous, honey," Carly reassured her. "You know what?" Carly turned to the kids who were sitting in the auditorium. "I bet everybody's a little nervous, right?" Nobody admitted it. "Right?" she said louder. "Anybody who is not at all nervous, raise your hand." There was some giggling, but no hands went up. "Okay, everybody get up on the stage. I want you to form a long line and follow me. Do whatever I do, got it?" The kids were lining up, but nobody answered. Carly put a hand behind each ear. "Got it?" she shouted.

"Got it!" they roared back, and I couldn't believe what happened next. Carly led the kids all over the stage. She would sing a line of a song, and they sang it back to her. Sometimes she sang it straight, and sometimes it was in a crazy voice or accent. Every now and then, she would speak a line of nonsense words. Some of the guys hung back at first, but she was so funny, only a couple of them were still rolling their eyes near the end, and she pulled in even them with a series of knock-knock jokes.

Finally she sent them all back to their seats and started in with the Wendys again. Amy was still the first one to audition, but she didn't look scared anymore, and she read without a single waver in her voice. Carly read the extra parts, using different voices for the characters, even a gruff one for Captain Hook. I could see how Carly could have been chosen for those lead roles in high school.

After Amy, there was a whole string of auditions by girls I didn't know—three of them named Emily. Some of them were pretty good, but most of them weren't great, even with a lot of encouragement by Carly.

When all the Wendys had finished, Carly jumped to her feet. "Thanks, ladies. That was very nice. Now, where are my Captain Hooks?"

A half dozen guys straggled onto the stage. Joel was about six inches taller than any of the others, which I thought might give him an advantage. Then he opened his mouth, and I knew he could have been seven feet tall and it wouldn't have helped. No wonder he wanted to bribe me to get the part. The guy on Gram's GPS had more expression in his voice than Joel.

At one point, Carly stopped him. "Try to sound a little more evil, Joel. Captain Hook is the bad guy, so nasty it up. You know what I mean?" Joel nodded, but then read with the exact same dull GPS voice. I saw Carly write something on her clipboard—probably not a compliment.

I looked around for Tenzie and saw her sitting at the far end of my row, studying her script. I hadn't thought to ask her what part she was trying out for. Then Carly announced, "Let's have all the Peter Pans onstage next," and I saw Tenzie follow a bunch of girls up the steps. Couldn't she see that Ashleigh Gianelli was in that group? If Ashleigh acted half as well as she looked, poor Tenzie didn't stand a chance. I felt bad for her because she really wanted to be in the play. She should have picked a small part.

Several girls were ahead of Tenzie in line, and they were all good—much better than any of the Wendys and Captain Hooks. Tenzie was just ahead of Ashleigh. I figured that was better than having to go after her and be humiliated.

When Tenzie walked to the center of the stage,

I could feel how scared she was. I was so worried about her, my mouth went dry. Why did she have to put herself through this? Why did she have to put *me* through this?

Then Tenzie took a deep breath, looked at the floor of the stage, and slowly raised her gaze until she was staring at something just above her eye level.

A kid a couple of rows behind me snorted, and his friends started laughing.

I checked to see if Tenzie had heard them, but she seemed perfectly calm. That's when I realized what she had done. She had built her magic grid right in front of everybody, and now she felt safe behind it. I could almost see it myself.

"Start whenever you're ready, Tenzie," Carly said.

As soon as Tenzie began speaking, she became Peter Pan. She strutted around the stage, hands on her hips, talking about not wanting to grow up. And then she broke into a song. Nobody else had done that. When she finished, a few kids even clapped.

Ashleigh Gianelli was up next. I had expected her to be better than Tenzie, but she overacted like crazy. I mean, I'm no expert, but she just looked silly, waving her arms around and making exaggerated faces. Then while I was sitting there, stunned, Ashleigh finished her audition and came to slip into the seat next to me. "Hi, Basil."

"Um, hi." She'd never said a word to me before.

"Was I completely terrible up there?" She batted her eyelashes at me. I'd never noticed before what long eyelashes she had. She smelled nice, too. Sort of flowery and spicy at the same time.

"No, you weren't *completely* terrible," I said. Ashleigh's eyebrows slammed together as if they had magnets attached to them. I realized I had said the wrong thing, so I added, "There were other kids worse than you." Now she was sitting on the edge of her seat, and her eyes were shooting sparks. I wasn't good at lying to people. What did they call it? Little white lies? Not easy! I tried one more time. "I mean almost everybody was worse than you."

Ashleigh relaxed and sat back in her seat. "*Almost* everybody? Who was better than me?"

"Well, Tenzie Verplank," I blurted out. I mean, it was so obvious, I figured that even Ashleigh must have realized Tenzie had the best audition.

She didn't. "Tenzie Verplank! You have to be kidding. That girl looks like a troll."

"She's the best actress," I said. "Acting isn't just about being beautiful, you know."

"You think I'm beautiful?" Ashleigh was back to her eyelash batting again. She didn't look half as pretty as before.

I didn't answer her. "I gotta go," I said, shouldering my backpack.

"Well, put in a good word for me with your mother, okay? I really want the lead in this play."

"Yeah, whatever." I couldn't believe it. I was blowing off the prettiest, most popular girl in the class.

I was almost to the door when Tenzie caught up to me. "Where are you going? You haven't tried out yet."

"I told you I'm not doing it," I said.

"I thought when you found out your mother was directing, you'd change your mind."

"Change my mind? Having Carly as the director makes it worse."

"I'm sorry, Basil."

"Sorry for what? It's not your fault that Carly is doing this."

"Well . . . it is sort of my fault. I told Mrs. Fischer about her being a Hollywood actress." Tenzie bit her lip. "Are you mad?"

I didn't know how to answer her. I didn't know what to think about much of anything anymore. "Gotta get home," I said, and took off. Halfway down the hall, I realized I never told Tenzie how great her audition was.

On the way out of school, I had to pass some kids who were talking in the hall. I recognized a couple of them who had been in the audition.

"Oooh, look," the big guy said. "Here comes the son of the Hollywood actress."

"Hey, Basil," a shorter kid said. "What part did you get? The lead?"

"I didn't try out," I mumbled, trying to get around them.

"I don't think his mother is a real actress at all," said a girl. "No real star would be hanging around Hayes Corners."

The big guy stepped out to block my way. "So is your mother just impersonating a famous star? She could go to jail for doing that, you know."

"Nobody said my mother is a star. She lived in Hollywood, and she's an actress, that's all." I pushed past him and ran for the door.

"Ooh, movie star's kid is too stuck up to talk with

us," he taunted. "Gotta go play with his rich actor buddies."

It felt good to get outside into the fresh air. I ran until I got out of breath, then walked the rest of the way home. It gave me time to think about what was happening to me. First Tenzie and now Carly attracted too much attention. And if I was around them, the spotlight landed on me, too.

Funny how the two things I used to wish for when I was younger were having a friend and having my mother come home. Now both wishes had come true, but Tenzie and Carly came with strings attached. I wanted things to go back to the way they were— uncomplicated—when everybody ignored me. After today, I would be the son of the movie star. No more hiding in the shadows. From what had just happened in the hall, I knew I was going to be miserable.

CHAPTER

12

The way it feels when the first cool weather arrives and you know summer isn't coming back—that's how it felt my next day at school. I didn't sense it right away, but first on the bus, then in the halls, I started to notice that people were looking at me. By the time I got to lunch, I knew I wasn't invisible anymore. I overheard somebody say, "That's Basil LeMay. His mother is a movie star."

Never mind that Charlize LeMay was a made-up name—because I guess Carly Feeney didn't sound "Hollywood" enough—but now I had inherited her phony last name, whether I liked it or not.

Carly must have sent someone in to post the call-back list because it was hanging on the front hall bulletin board first thing in the morning. I took a quick peek and saw that Tenzie was on the list, but I didn't see Joel and Ashleigh. I figured that meant Tenzie was still in the running and the other two weren't.

All through lunch period, kids who had never spoken to me before were acting as if we were best friends. Did they think a thirty-second small-talk conversation would make me forget they'd been ignoring me since the beginning of the school year?

Ashleigh Gianelli came up to me in the hall. "Did you tell her?"

"Tell who what?" I asked.

Ashleigh threw her head back in a lame imitation of a laugh. "Tell your mother about what a great Peter Pan I'd be, silly. Just in case she has the slightest little smidgen of a doubt." She planted a kiss in the air in the general vicinity of my cheek and took off.

"Yeah, okay. I will," I mumbled to her back. Maybe it wouldn't hurt to say something to Carly. After all, Tenzie was a good actress. She'd get a part just from talent alone, without any help from me.

A few minutes later, I spotted Joel Mack across the

cafeteria. When he saw me, he grinned and pantomimed tossing a football to me. Then he gave me a thumbs-up. I'd better talk to Carly about him tonight, too. I didn't want to be on his football team, but he wasn't the kind of guy I wanted to have mad at me.

Was this what it was like to be popular? I was the same person everybody had been ignoring all along, and suddenly I was worth knowing because of my mother. It was annoying, but I was surprised that it felt kind of good to be noticed for a change.

I didn't go to see the callback auditions at the end of the day. Instead, I hung around in shop to finish up Gram's game cabinet. I rubbed it all over one last time to polish up the stain, then put the door fastener on. I was pretty impressed with the way it came out. I couldn't wait to give it to Gram.

The cabinet was awkward to carry, but I managed to get it on the bus. It just fit on the seat beside me. A bunch of kids crowded around to ask me about it. One kid said, "No way you made that by yourself. It looks like it came from a store." He didn't know that Gram and I thought handmade things were ten times better than store-bought. But I could tell he meant it as a compliment, so I thanked him.

The driver closed the door, and the late bus lurched into motion. I looked around and saw that most of the kids on the bus had probably come from the drama club callbacks, but I didn't see Tenzie.

When I got home, Carly was already there. She had pictures and index cards with notes spread out on the table. She looked up. "Hi, Basil. What's that thing you're carrying?"

"It's a cabinet for Gram to put her board games in."

Carly smiled and shook her head. "Is she still playing those old things? I thought she might have moved up to video games by now, but I guess she's stuck with her old-fashioned ways. Where'd you get the cabinet?"

"We both like board games," I said. "And I didn't *get* the cabinet anywhere. I made it in school."

Carly got up and came over to run her hand over the wood. "Really? You made this? I'm impressed, Basil. I didn't know they taught these skills in school."

"I've done stuff like this with Gram for years," I said.

Carly nodded. "Yes, Mom can make just about anything. I guess I didn't inherit that kind of talent."

"I'm going to hide this in my room for now," I said. "It's a surprise, so don't tell her." Since I had missed

Gram's birthday, it didn't really matter when I gave it to her, but I wanted to do it when Carly wasn't around. It felt good to have her praise me for building the cabinet, and I liked hearing her say something nice about Gram, but I still didn't like having her live here.

I didn't go back into the kitchen until I heard Gram and Carly talking.

Gram turned when she heard me. "Oh, I didn't know you were home. How was school?"

"Okay, I guess." I sat at the opposite end of the table from Carly. "Are these the kids who got in the play?"

"I'm still making the final decisions, Basil."

Gram came to look over Carly's shoulder. "This play seems like a huge job. Are you sure you can handle it?"

Carly let out a sharp breath. "What do you think I was doing the whole time I was in California, Mom? I could run an audition in my sleep."

Gram picked up a couple of kids' pictures. "I'm not talking about the audition. I'm worried about what comes afterward—rehearsals, scenery, costumes, and putting together the final production. You've never been very good at following through on your projects, Carly, and these eager young faces are counting on you."

Carly snatched the pictures from Gram. "Do you mind? I had these all in order. And I wouldn't have started this if I didn't know I could pull it off. Please leave me alone."

"Fine!" Gram headed back for her studio.

I pulled my chair closer so I could check out the pictures, but I didn't see Ashleigh, Joel, or Tenzie.

"How about Ashleigh Gianelli?" I asked.

Carly slapped a card and picture onto what seemed to be her discard pile. Go Fish! Another actor's dream bites the dust. "I don't remember an Ashleigh. What part did she try out for?"

"Peter Pan."

Carly shuffled through a small pile of pictures, then looked up. "Nope, I don't have her in the final selections. Must be she didn't make an impression. Is she a friend of yours?"

"Sort of," I said.

"Well, I'd like to give parts to your friends, Basil, but that's really not fair. We shouldn't even be talking about this. You'll find out who got the parts tomorrow when the cast list gets posted."

That took care of Ashleigh. After all, I did mention her name to Carly. I had a great excuse not to be on

Joel's football team, too. But what about Tenzie? I opened my mouth to ask, then decided not to. If her picture wasn't there, I was afraid I knew the answer.

✦ ✦ ✦

Tenzie was on the bus the next morning, but couldn't sit with me because a girl I recognized from the first audition had slipped in beside me. The girl rode along in silence for a while, then surprised me by asking, "Is your mother going to post the cast list today?"

"I don't know," I said.

"Have you seen it?" She leaned forward so she could look into my face.

"Seen what?"

She sighed. "The cast list."

"No, I saw her working on it, is all."

"Did you notice if there was an Emily on the list?" she asked, twisting the strap on her backpack.

I knew there had to be an Emily on the list, because one out of every four or five girls in our class was named Emily. "Yeah, I think I saw an Emily."

She flashed me a big smile. "Oh, thank you!"

I was glad Emily didn't ask about the last name. This way she could hope she was on the list until she saw it. Who knew? She might have a part. And I liked the fact that she didn't ask me to help her get it.

I was Mr. Popular from the minute I stepped off the bus—people waving to me and high-fiving me in the hall. In the three minutes it took to get to my homeroom, I heard my name called out more times than I had since school started in September. Actually, I didn't remember hearing anybody call out my name before.

A bunch of kids came over to our desk at lunch. I should say my desk, because Tenzie wasn't there. She wasn't there in math class at first, but she slid in right before the bell. She turned in her seat. "Have you seen the cast list?"

"No, is it up yet? Did you make it?"

"We'll see after class."

The evil eye from Mrs. Lowe ended our conversation.

At the end of class, Tenzie bolted out of the room before I could gather up my books. As I headed for the front hall, I got a pretty good preview of who was on the list and who wasn't. A few kids were still friendly, but some were glaring at me, and a couple of them knocked into me on purpose. One girl bumped me so hard, I dropped my books all over the floor. As I was on my knees gathering my stuff, a big foot landed on my notebook. I looked up—way up—to the face of Joel Mack.

"Thanks a bunch, you little twerp. You said you'd help us get the parts, and you didn't. I don't care about me, but Ashleigh really wanted the part."

Ashleigh Gianelli was clinging to his arm, crying. "You lied, Basil."

I tried to ease my notebook out from under Joel's mammoth sneaker. "I did mention your name. It didn't do any good."

The Neanderthal foot moved and slammed down harder, almost trapping some fingers this time. "So Ashleigh's such a bad actress that no amount of pleading with your mother got her the part. Is that what you're saying?"

That made Ashleigh start snuffling louder. I knew there was no good answer to that question, so I kept my mouth shut. I felt myself being pulled to my feet by my shirt collar. I also felt something rip. "Don't even think about showing up for my football league," Joel snarled as he dropped me.

"Oh, believe me, I won't," I whispered to a floor tile.

After I checked for a broken nose and got myself together, I moved along close to the wall, trying not to notice the people who were glaring at me. Then I realized most of them weren't noticing me at all. Was I on my way to becoming a nobody again?

There was a small crowd clustered around the bulletin board. I edged my way in, then I saw it—PETER PAN: TENZIE VERPLANK.

I couldn't help grinning.

Then I felt Tenzie poke my elbow. "Did you see?"

"Yeah. Congratulations."

"Thanks. You didn't know ahead of time?"

"No, Carly wouldn't tell me anything. I was worried because she had all these kids' pictures spread out on the table last night, and I didn't see yours."

"She never took my picture," Tenzie said. "She didn't need to because she already knew me."

That made sense. "I haven't seen you since the audition," I said. "Were you mad at me for not trying out?"

"No. I know this isn't your thing. I just didn't want to hang around you and Carly while she was deciding on the cast."

"I wish everybody had been like that."

She laughed. "You got pretty popular for a while there."

"For about forty-eight hours," I said. "Just long enough to figure out that I don't want to be popular."

"Good, now you can go back to being unpopular with me."

"Are you kidding? You're the star of the show. You won't want to hang around with me anymore."

She struck a dramatic pose. "You're right. Divas can't be seen with mere humans." She punched me on the arm. "Come on. We're going to miss the bus. Hey, did you know you have a big rip in the back of your shirt?"

"Really?" I said. "I have no idea how that happened."

CHAPTER

13

When I got into the house, Carly was on the phone. "Yes, your daughter is lovely, Mrs. Lansing, but her acting ability . . ." Carly rolled her eyes at me, then turned her back. I could just barely hear somebody yelling on the phone. Carly kept trying to get a word in, but couldn't find an opening. "I'm . . . I'm sorry you feel . . . Mrs. Lansing. I'm sure Lisa . . . could do a fine job in the chorus . . . then next year, with some experience—" Carly looked at her cell phone for a second, then flipped it closed. "She hung up on me!"

"Was that the mother of somebody who didn't get a part?" I asked.

"Yes. It was the fourth call from an irate parent."

"Why don't you turn off your phone?" I asked.

Carly shook her head. "An actor never turns off her phone. You never know when somebody might be calling with the big break."

It seemed odd that Carly was saying no to people on one hand while she was hoping for a yes on the other.

I started to go into my room when Carly stopped me. "Basil, I need you to do me a favor."

I noticed she was telling, not asking.

She handed me a notebook. "This is for taking notes at rehearsals."

"But I'm not in the play."

"You'll be my assistant," she said. "Write down notes to remind me of things I need to do."

I tried to give her back the notebook. "I don't know anything about plays. I wouldn't have a clue what to write down."

"I'll tell you what to write, Basil. Just be there. Please?" She was as good at the puppy-dog expression as Tenzie. "I really need your help."

I decided to go along with Carly, mainly because

the play meant so much to Tenzie. If I could help make it better, I would be doing her a favor, not Carly.

Carly's phone rang again. "Hello?" From the expression on her face, I could tell that this was not somebody calling with her big break.

+ + +

I sat through the Monday and Wednesday rehearsals, where all I wrote in the notebook were the dates—10/15, 10/17—and a bunch of doodles. So far, Carly hadn't given me any notes at all. At least I didn't think she had. Writing down the numbers always sent me off into thoughts about their colors, like the fact that October was ten, or in my system one and zero, which were both white. This number seemed more appropriate for a winter month with snow, not October, when the trees were a blaze of four, five, and three/six.

The Friday rehearsal was only for the leads. It was the first time Carly pulled out the music. "Okay, everybody, we're going to learn a song called 'Tender Shepherd.' Mrs. Darling and her children, Wendy, John, and Michael, take the stage. Tenzie, you can sit this one out. We'll work on your solo after the others have left."

Two guys and two girls shuffled up onto the stage, and Tenzie slipped into the seat beside me.

"Does anybody know this song?" Carly asked.

They all shook their heads.

"All right," Carly said. "I need somebody to play the melody on the piano to get us started. Who can do that for me?"

The kids on the stage looked at each other and shrugged.

Carly walked over to the piano. "Okay, I'll plunk it out." She sat on the piano bench, scowling at the music, her index finger hovering over the keyboard like a helicopter trying to find a safe place to land.

"Does your mother know how to play the piano?" Tenzie whispered.

"How should I know?" I whispered back.

"Well, it doesn't matter. She's a fabulous director. Didn't you love the way she got everybody to relax at the audition? You're so lucky to have such a cool mother, Basil."

Maybe Carly had been cool at the auditions, but I sure wouldn't have called her a fabulous director now. She played a few notes on the piano, then said, "No, wait," and made a motion with her hand as if to erase the notes from the air.

After a few more false starts, Tenzie jumped to her feet. "I can't play the piano, but I know the song. Want me to sing it for them, Miss LeMay?"

Carly gave her a bright smile. "That would be terrific, Tenzie. Come on up here."

I couldn't believe Carly called a whole rehearsal to work on music and was just hoping one of the kids would be able to play the piano. Planning ahead sure wasn't her strong point. But I was the only one bothered by it. With Tenzie's help, Carly was working her magic just the way she did at the audition, and I could tell all the kids thought she was wonderful.

Tenzie got her starting note from the piano, then sang the melody through with a clear voice.

"Perfect," Carly declared. "Now this song is a round, so you'll all be singing the same melody—just starting it at different points. Let's try having you all sing along with Tenzie this time."

It sounded pretty good, except for Alison, the girl playing Wendy. She couldn't carry a tune and hadn't even started on the right note.

"Tenzie, why don't you stand next to Alison so she can hear you," Carly said.

They tried it several times, but Alison just got worse. "I never could sing," Alison said. "I didn't even know this was going to be a musical." She looked as if she were going to cry.

"It's fine," Carly said. "We don't have to have a singing Wendy. Just mouth the words in this song. We can have you speak the words to your solos. Nobody will know the difference."

When Tenzie came back to sit next to me, I asked, "How much does Wendy have to sing in this play?"

"A lot," she said, folding her arms and sliding down in her seat. "She's one of the main singing parts."

At the next rehearsal, we found out that Captain Hook couldn't carry a tune either. And the girl playing Tiger Lily—a part for a dancer—had two left feet. When I mentioned this to Tenzie, she wasn't worried. "Those kids might not be great singers or dancers, but Carly chose the best actors. That's what counts. The music stuff is just to fill in."

I decided to give Carly the benefit of the doubt. After all, she had a lot of experience. She must have a plan. Tenzie had gone to a school where they had plays all the time. If she thought Carly was doing a good job, I wasn't going to worry.

But then there were a couple more disastrous rehearsals. We found out there were no kids with any artistic talent on the scenery crew. Even worse, Carly kept changing her mind about blocking—where she wanted kids to move around onstage—so nobody could remember where they were supposed to go. I had notes crossed out, written over, and crossed out again. Some kids were starting to say that Carly didn't know what she was doing. The magic wasn't working anymore.

✦ ✦ ✦

After Friday's rehearsal, I ran out and got on the late bus so I wouldn't have to ride with Carly. I hadn't been home for more than a few minutes when Carly came into the house. "Basil, I need you to help me with something. Meet me out in the barn."

"Okay. Give me a minute. I have to do some stuff first." I was stalling. What would Carly be doing in the barn? There was nothing out there but chickens and Gram's welding equipment. Whatever she wanted, I wished I had come up with an excuse when she asked me. I was never good at thinking fast on my feet. I hung out in the house until I heard Carly yelling, "Basil, get out here. I can't wait around all day!"

"What do you want me to do?" I asked. As I got closer to the barn, I saw a length of clothesline hanging over a barn rafter. That gave me chills until I made sure it didn't have a noose at one end.

Then Carly said something just as scary. "Tenzie has to soar above the stage as Peter Pan. I'm going to have her come over and try out this flying harness, but I'm going to use you as the guinea pig first."

She held out a thing made of leather straps. I couldn't picture how a person could be hauled up in the air in it, but I'd seen enough of Carly in action to know that she hadn't really thought out the safety angle. Still, my own mother wouldn't do anything to hurt me, would she?

"How do you put it on?" I asked.

"Stick one foot through here and the other one through here."

I followed her directions. She yanked the thing up and tightened the top part around my waist. The holes for the legs were uneven, so one side hung almost to my knee and the other one fit like a tourniquet.

"This doesn't feel right," I said. "Is it upside down?"

"No, this is the only way I can make it work." She tugged at the loose leg strap, but couldn't tighten it up.

"Where did you get this thing?" I asked. "It doesn't even look like it's made for a person."

"Don't be so critical, Basil. I got it on eBay, and if you must know, it's for a Great Dane." She grabbed one end of the clothesline that was hanging over a barn rafter and started tying it to the waistband of the harness.

"Wait a minute. You're going to haul me up in the air in a dog harness?"

"This harness is brand-new, so it's never been on a dog, okay?" Carly tied knot after clumsy knot, until the end of the clothesline looked like one of Gram's macramé plant hangers. Then she put on a pair of old leather gloves, and before I knew what was happening, she reached up high to grab the other end of the rope and put her whole weight into pulling it down.

"Hang on. Here we go."

"Whoa!" I shouted, as my feet left the ground and I felt the most painful wedgie of my life. "Let me down!" I screeched, but Carly jumped up to get a higher hand-hold and wrenched me soaring toward the rafter. Then my body flipped over, so I was head down, slipping out of the harness. I kicked and frantically wrapped my legs around the rafter as all the blood in my body collected in my head.

"What are you doing?" Carly yelled. "You're supposed to stay upright."

"Oh, excuse me," I shouted. "I missed your careful instructions." The floor of the barn looked miles away.

"Stop kidding around, Basil. I mean it. Reach up and grab the rafter with your hands."

I tried to stretch for the rafter, but I didn't have the strength to move. I had seen kids on the playground hanging from the overhead pole by their knees, then folding up to hang by their hands. They made it look easy, but whatever muscles it took to do that must have been left out of my body from birth. All I could do was waggle a little bit, but no way were my hands getting up to that rafter.

The edges of the board were cutting into my legs. How much longer could I hang on? For a moment, time seemed to go into slow motion. I've heard that's what happens to some people just before they die. I could see Carly below me pacing in circles, waving her hands around. She looked small and helpless. This was the mother I'd dreamed of all those years? The one I hoped would come home and take care of me?

Carly's screech jolted me back. "Basil, you're going to fall!"

"I know!" I yelled.

"What's going on in here?" I saw an upside-down Gram in the doorway.

"Mom, make Basil stop fooling around."

Gram sprung into action. She grabbed a wooden ladder that was leaning against the wall, but when she tried to prop it against the rafter, it was about three feet too short.

"He's going to die!" Carly sobbed.

"Stop blubbering and help me with this ladder, Carly."

Carly was too far gone. All she could do was fan her face with both hands while Gram struggled to position the ladder on an upright beam a few feet away from me.

"Basil, you have to grab hold of that rafter so you can get over to the ladder," Gram said.

I made another attempt to fold myself up, but it was no use. "I can't do it."

"Yes, you can." Gram was holding the ladder steady.

"Let your body swing a couple of times to get you in range," Gram said.

"I can't!" I yelled again. My head was dizzy from being clogged up with blood. I pictured all that blood splattering over the concrete barn floor when I lost my grip and my skull split open like a Halloween pumpkin.

Gram must have seen the same picture because she picked up a huge armload of hay and dumped it on the floor below me.

"You want me to let go and land on that?"

"No, I want you to hang on for dear life until I get the fire department here. This is just in case."

"Wait!" I yelled. Maybe it was the image of being rescued like a kitten stuck in a tree or picturing the story on the local TV station that everybody would laugh at, but something made my body start working again. I made a couple of tentative swings, then with a sudden surge of confidence, I had the skills of a trapeze artist. Well, that's an exaggeration, but at least I wasn't frozen in place anymore. The third swing got my hands within a foot of the rafter, and with the next swing, I got close enough to wrap my arms around it. Now I was suspended like a monkey, hanging by both arms and legs with my head toward the ladder but still a good five or six feet away from it.

"He's stuck," Carly whined.

"No, I'm not!"

I had to mentally tell each body part how to move me across that rafter, sliding first one arm, then the other, then skootching my legs along to catch up.

"Good job, Basil," Gram called up to me. "You're lined up with the ladder now. If you hang on tight with your arms, you can let your legs down to reach the top rung."

I closed my eyes, hugged the rafter with all my strength, and let go with my legs. I felt around with my feet, but couldn't find the ladder. For a few panicked seconds, I thought I was going to fall after all.

"A little more to the right," Gram said. Her voice sounded closer. When I peeked out of one eye, I saw that she was several steps up on the ladder. She grabbed my right foot and placed it on the top rung.

"Thanks, Gram. I've got it from here," I said. Gram had been there for me my whole life, but this went way beyond anything she'd ever done. It wasn't lost on me that my mother was totally useless in an emergency.

I was still scared until I could hold on to the sides

of the ladder with my hands. When I was safely on the floor, I stepped out of the harness and turned to Carly. "This was a crazy idea."

"I just need to solve a few problems," Carly said. "I know I can make it work."

"Yeah, sure," I said. "As long as you replace Tenzie with a Great Dane."

Gram pulled the harness out of Carly's hands. "Whoa. This is how you were going to make Peter Pan fly?"

"Well, not exactly," Carly said. "This was only a trial run."

"Trial run! Basil could have been killed."

"Don't be so dramatic, Mother. Nothing happened to Basil."

"No thanks to you," Gram said. "You can't just rig something on your own, Carly. Go look up companies who make flying harnesses for theaters."

"I didn't think of it, okay?"

"I bet Mrs. Fischer made arrangements to get a real flying harness," I said. "Just like she would have asked the music teacher to direct the singing. Did you even bother to check?" The fact that my own mother had just put my life at risk was beginning to sink in.

Carly glared at me. "No, I did not check with Mrs. Fischer or the music teacher, okay? Are you two done yelling at me now? Because if you're not, I'm going to drop this whole project. I'm getting criticized by everybody. I don't need grief from my own family." She turned and headed for the house.

"Wait!" I yelled, running after Carly. She was already in the kitchen by the time I caught up to her. "You're not really thinking of quitting the play, are you? Tenzie has been working so hard on learning her lines, I think she has the whole thing memorized."

Carly was collecting her papers into a pile at the end of the kitchen table. Gram came through the door. "This is just like you, Carly. I had a feeling when you started this project that you'd cut out before you fin-ished it."

Carly slammed her hand on the table. "You don't understand what a huge job this is. I never should have agreed to direct the play in the first place."

I was so mad at Carly, I could hardly see straight. She had swept into my life, taken over Gram and my best friend, and made herself into a big deal at school. And now that she had everybody fired up about the play, she was thinking of quitting? Kids were upset with me for not getting them a part. Now the kids who did get into the play would probably blame me for Carly dropping out—especially Tenzie. Her magic grid couldn't protect her from this disappointment. I started for my room, but I'd still hear Carly and Gram fighting from there. I had to get out of the house.

CHAPTER 14

I ran down the road and didn't stop until I was out of breath. I didn't care where I went, but the running helped to clear my head. I turned off the main road and started up the dirt road that climbed to the top of a small hill. This was where I used to go to watch the first stages of construction at Elegant Acres on the next hill over. There was an old tree stump that made a good spot to sit and think. I could see the top floor of what I figured was Tenzie's house and wondered if she was home yet. Should I tell her about Carly maybe leaving the play? It would be better than waiting until she heard it from somebody else.

I spotted a small path that wound down the hill toward Elegant Acres. It hadn't been here in the old days. I didn't know if it would take me all the way over to Tenzie's, but it was worth a try. The path headed in the right direction, then came to an end at a crumbling stone wall. Beyond that were some dense woods that didn't seem to have a path going through them, so I went back to my tree stump, where I could sit and figure out what to do next.

As I looked across to Elegant Acres, I saw somebody—a kid—leaving the development and starting down the hill. I squinted to see if it was anybody I recognized from school. At first I couldn't make out the face or even tell if it was a boy or a girl. Then I recognized the bounce in the walk and knew it was Tenzie. I watched her jump over a log that had fallen across the path, then continue down into the hollow between the two hills. Pretty soon, she disappeared behind the woods. I didn't think she could get up here from there, but a few minutes later, she appeared at the edge of the woods and climbed over the stone wall.

"Hey, Basil!" she called. She was wearing the Peter Pan hat that Gram had found for her in our costume closet. I started to panic. I hadn't worked out how to tell her about Carly and the play. Maybe I should wait until it was definite. I got up and started walking fast toward the road, pretending I hadn't heard her.

She kept yelling and getting closer, and since I couldn't run without making it obvious that I was trying to get away from her, I finally stopped and waited for her to catch up.

"What are you doing out here? I saw you from my bedroom window."

"I was taking a walk."

"What's wrong? You look upset."

This was the trouble with having a friend, especially a girl. "You look upset" is not something a guy would say. At least I never would. "Carly and Gram are having a fight."

"What are they fighting about?"

"The play." The words slipped out of my mouth.

"What does Gram have to do with the play?"

"Nothing! Forget it." I started walking home. I felt like a cornered animal. No matter which way I turned, I was heading for trouble.

"Wait!" Tenzie grabbed my arm. "Carly's not going to quit the play, is she?"

"I don't know. I . . . No! Why would you think that?"

"I bet anything she's thinking of dropping the play," Tenzie said, picking up the pace. "I've had a funny feeling about that for the past week. Carly doesn't seem to know what she's doing, so I've been afraid she'd give up. But we could help her pull everything together, Basil. I know we could. Come on, let's talk to her."

I tried to hang back. "I never said anything about her quitting. Where are you getting all these crazy ideas?"

"You're not good at hiding things, Basil. It's written all over your face."

I always thought Gram could read my mind, but Tenzie knew what I was thinking even when I wasn't so sure myself. Before I could stop her, Tenzie had taken off running toward my house, and she had too much of a head start for me to catch up.

Tenzie knocked at the door instead of barging in, so I got there just as Gram opened it. "Hi, Tenzie, I haven't seen you for a few days," Gram said.

"I've been busy with the play, Gram." Even though Tenzie had been hanging out at our house for a while now, it still bothered me to hear her call my grandmother Gram.

Carly quickly wiped tears from her cheeks, and Gram's face was red enough to be sunburned. I wondered what awful things they had said to each other while I was gone.

Gram slipped into hostess mode and started digging through the cupboard. "Would you kids like a snack? I think I have some popcorn."

"I'm not hungry," Tenzie said, stepping in front of Carly. "What's going on with the play? You're not going to quit, are you?"

Carly glared at me. "Basil, what did you tell her?"

"Nothing! I didn't say a word. I just—"

Tenzie put up her hand to shush me. "He didn't have to tell me anything. I figured it out on my own. Look, I know the play is a ton of work, but Basil and I will help you out more, make things easier on you." She looked over her shoulder at me. "Right, Basil?"

"Yeah, I guess."

Tenzie turned to Carly. "You just name it, Carly. Let us know what you need, and it's done." She grabbed my rehearsal notebook off the table and turned to a blank page. "I'll make a list right now. C'mon, what's the first thing you need us to do?"

Carly smiled and put her hand on Tenzie's arm. "I really appreciate this, Tenzie, but it's a little more complicated. It's not that I want to quit directing the play. It looks like I'll have to go back to Hollywood. Something unexpected came up. It could be a real opportunity for me."

Gram slammed the microwave popcorn bag down on the table. It ripped open, spilling kernels all over the floor. "Tell them the truth, Carly. You always split when the going gets tough."

My brain was slow to take in Carly's words. Quit directing the play. Okay, I was expecting that. But what was the other part? Have to go back to Hollywood? Unexpected? Real opportunity? "Let me get this straight. You're dumping me again?"

"Don't be so dramatic, Basil." Carly fidgeted with a sparkly pin in her hair. "This just came up, and I have to go out to LA."

I planted myself right in front of Carly. "What came up? You're getting a part in a big movie? You're going to be a star?"

Carly's eyes shifted away from mine as she moved back a couple of steps. "It's nothing definite yet."

I wasn't buying any of this. "It's nothing, period, right? It's just an excuse to get away from the mess you've made. An excuse to leave me again?"

Carly was still avoiding eye contact with me. "Basil,

you're being completely self-centered. This isn't about you."

"It sure feels like it's about me. You deserted me when I was an adorable little kid. It should be even easier to take off now that I'm not so cute anymore, right?"

Carly spun around to face me. "Hold it! Is that what my mother told you? That I deserted you?"

"That's pretty much it," I said. "Do you have any other explanation?"

"I can't believe this. Okay, if you've been told a bunch of lies, you're going to hear the truth now." Carly grasped me by the shoulders. Her face was so close to mine, I could see the little gold dots in the blue irises of her eyes that made them look green from a distance. "I didn't leave you here because I wanted to, Basil. Your grandmother convinced me that she could take better care of you than I could. She said when I made it big and could support you, I could come home and get you."

"Gram, she's lying, isn't she?"

Carly was staring Gram down. "Tell him, Mom. You sure had plenty to say back then, about how it wasn't fair of me to take Basil away from a stable home. How you could give him love and security, and I couldn't. I cried and cried and said I couldn't leave my baby behind." Carly's voice got higher, sharper. "Do you even remember that, Mom, or have you told the lie to yourself so many times you believe I was the one at fault?"

I looked at Gram, but she couldn't meet my eyes. Her silence was the only answer I needed. "How could I be so stupid?" I yelled, and for the second time that day, I slammed out of the house.

+ + +

I stood outside for a few minutes, trying to get my thoughts together, then Tenzie came running out. "Basil, you have to do something."

"Me? I'm not even in the play. Somebody else will take over. Maybe the music teacher or one of the other parents."

"I'm not talking about the play." She put her hand on my shoulder. "You have to stop Carly from leaving. Let's go to my house and make a plan."

"How can I do that? Nobody ever listens to me, especially her. We barely know each other. Besides, I don't even want her to stay." I picked up a rock on the side of the road and lobbed it toward Gram's garden. A startled rabbit exploded out of the teepee of pole beans and streaked for the cover of the woods. I knew exactly how he felt.

We waited for a few cars to go by, then headed across the road to Elegant Acres.

"While I was in there, Carly called the station asking when the next bus left."

"Next bus to where?"

"All she said was the next westbound bus."

"Why would she say that? Why didn't she ask about the bus to Hollywood?"

Tenzie raised her eyebrows. "I don't think there is a bus that goes from Broxburg to Hollywood. You probably have to go a lot of places in between with different buses."

Of course she was right. I could feel my face go red. As we trudged through the development, there was no sign of life, as usual. Even the dogs seemed to be inside, their secret fences guarding nothing but insects and maybe a few chipmunks.

"I know what I would do if I were you," Tenzie mumbled.

I didn't take her bait. My life was a total mess, and I didn't want anybody's advice on how to fix it. I just wanted to wallow in my misery.

Tenzie wasn't giving up. "If I had a mother who loved me as much as Carly loves you, I'd do anything to keep her with me."

"Yeah, she loves me so much, she's taking off again."

Tenzie gave me a shove that almost knocked me off my feet. "Weren't you listening back there? She wanted to take you the first time, but your grandmother wouldn't let her."

"Oh, so now she's *my grandmother*? What happened to calling her Gram?"

"I'm mad at her. She cheated you out of growing up with your real mother. But you haven't exactly been a loving son, either. Since Carly came back, you've criticized every move she made. Between you and your grandmother, it's no wonder she wants to get out of here. I would too, if I were her."

We reached Tenzie's house and went inside. Nobody was home, as usual. Tenzie threw her books on the kitchen island. "I have to call Mom and let her know I'm home."

Tenzie was right. I hadn't been all that nice to Carly. But I was having a hard time believing that Gram had been lying to me all those years. She was the only family I'd ever known. She didn't have to fight to keep me. She could've let Carly drag me across the country.

Tenzie slid her phone across the island. "I don't know why I bother to do that. The days I forget to call, Mom never mentions it. Both of them leave for work before I'm up. Half the time, my mother leaves a frozen dinner for me to microwave, and I'm in bed by the time either of them get home. You're lucky to have a mother who cares about you. I could be gone for a week before my parents even noticed."

"This Carly thing isn't as simple as you're making it out to be. If Carly wanted me with her, why didn't she come back for me?"

"You heard your grandmother. She said the deal was for Carly to come back for you after she was a success in Hollywood, but that never happened. Can you imagine how humiliating it was for Carly to admit she failed?" Tenzie looked out the window for a minute, then she turned to me. "Give Carly a break, Basil. She wanted to be with you, so she came home in spite of everything. Let's go back and talk her out of leaving."

This was all moving too fast for me. "I . . . I don't think—"

Tenzie grabbed my shoulders and turned me to face the door. "Good. Don't think. Thinking is highly overrated."

Every time I tried to come up with an argument on the way to my house, Tenzie shushed me. She was the bossiest girl I'd ever met. I had no idea why I even liked her. Maybe I didn't like her. But she was the only friend I had.

This time we went into my house together. Gram was at the kitchen table wrapping sun catchers to send out. From the way she was shoving the bubble wrap into the box, I could tell she was in a bad mood.

"Where's Carly?" I asked.

"Gone," Gram said.

"Gone where?" Tenzie and I said, almost in unison.

"I wouldn't know. She didn't let me in on her plans."

I ran to Carly's room. All her clothes and other things were missing, not that there had been much in the first place. The only signs of her were a notepad on the desk and a couple of sparkly hairpins on the floor.

Tenzie was behind me, breathing down my neck. "How could she pack up so fast?"

As I clung to the doorjamb, a picture of Carly's

room flashed through my mind—her two purple suit-cases on the floor, overflowing with clothes. "I don't think she ever really unpacked," I whispered. I tried to hold back the tears as we went into the kitchen. "She left without even saying good-bye," I said, sink-ing into one of the kitchen chairs.

Gram looked up without smiling. "I'm sorry, Basil. Carly has always done what she wants when she wants. Doesn't matter who she hurts."

"But she wanted to take me with her when she left the first time, and you wouldn't let her," I said.

"You didn't hear that conversation, Basil. You've only got her side of it."

"Well, what's your side, Gram? Did Carly beg to take me now? Did you say she had to leave me here again?"

Gram snapped off a piece of tape and plastered it on the sun catcher box. "Believe me, you're better off without her."

Tenzie grabbed my arm. "C'mon, Basil. I need you to help carry my stuff home."

I started to ask what stuff when her fingers dug into my flesh. "Oh, yeah, your stuff." I followed her out the door.

Tenzie shushed me from talking until we got far

enough across the yard so Gram couldn't hear through the window.

"What do you want?" I asked finally.

"I'm going with you," she said.

"I'm not going anywhere."

"Yes you are, Basil. Your grandmother lied to you again. She sent your mother off without you."

"Carly could have taken me along if she really wanted to."

"I don't think so. Did you see how mad your grandmother looked? I just know they had the same fight they did years ago. I bet Carly begged to take you with her and your grandmother refused. Carly loves you, Basil."

"I don't want to talk about this anymore." I ducked my head so she couldn't see my face.

"All right. We're wasting time anyway. Go inside and pack as many clothes as you can fit into your school backpack, but don't let your grandmother see you do it. Do you have any money?"

I pictured the jar on my desk that had a few spare coins in it. "Not really."

"Bring what you have," Tenzie said. "I've saved over a hundred fifty dollars from my allowance."

"Really? How could you save that much? My allowance is usually gone by the end of the week."

Tenzie shrugged. "I don't like to shop, and it made me feel good knowing I had money in case I ever needed to get away—like now. Tomorrow morning tell your grandmother you're walking to school, then go up over the hill and come down the back path to my house."

"But I don't get it," I said. "What are we doing?"

Tenzie sighed. "Basil, don't be such a doofus. We're going to follow your mother."

"We're running away from home?"

Tenzie scowled. "What home? Nobody here cares about either one of us."

My mind was swimming with questions. "How can we find Carly? Won't people be looking for us?"

"No. Remember the day I walked out of school? They don't check on us as much as you think. Search Carly's room for clues about where she lived. See if she wrote anything in that notepad on her desk. I'll do an Internet search on her name—both of them—to see what I can find out, then I'll check bus schedules."

None of it made any sense, but Tenzie was right about one thing. Neither one of us had anybody here who really cared about us. We had nothing to lose.

CHAPTER 15

When I went into the house, I could hear Gram's *Sgt. Pepper* album coming from the hippie room, which told me that she had gone up to the loft to work on her stained glass. It also told me she was upset, because she usually used Beatles music to cheer herself up. That would probably keep her occupied long enough for me to look for clues and pack up the stuff I needed to take with me. I decided to check out Carly's room first, because I didn't want Gram to catch me in there. I could pretend I was doing homework in my room later while I packed.

I thumbed through the notepad on the desk. There was nothing written in it. Then I pulled out the drawer and found it stuffed with papers that had Carly's handwriting on them. There had to be something in here, but it was going to take some time to go through it. Gram's music was still playing, so I dove into the papers.

There were a lot of notes to herself, mostly about the play. I could tell that some of them had been written at the rehearsal, but others were longer, working out what she wanted to do the next day—new ideas she wanted to try out. The way Carly had acted so scattered at rehearsals, I was surprised that she had put so much thought into the play.

There were a couple of notes that didn't fit with the rest. One said, *Find out where Alex and Grace are living now.* The other was *Spend more time with Basil.* It made me mad that Carly needed to remind herself to spend more time with me. But I couldn't help feeling a little pleased that she had thought about me at all. How pathetic was that?

The rest of the stuff in the drawer was the pictures of kids from the audition and index cards with notes she had taken about them. I closed the drawer and put my head down on the desk. There wasn't a single clue that Tenzie and I could use. In a way, that was a relief, because running after Carly had sounded like a bad idea from the start. I was about to go call Tenzie and tell her that I had failed, when looking sideways across the notepad from my head-on-the-desk perspective, I saw some impressions in the paper. I turned on the desk lamp, then held the notepad up close to it, tilting the pad from side to side until the light hit the indentations just right. Sure enough, it was writing, made from the pressure of a pen. Carly had written something on the top sheet and then torn it off the pad.

I remembered an old movie that Gram and I had watched, where somebody brought up the words of a letter on a blank sheet of notepaper with indentations just like this one. They did it by rubbing the side of a soft pencil across the paper. I took the pad into my room and rummaged through my desk for the right kind of pencil. I started out by pressing too hard, and flattened out some of the writing. Then I rubbed the side of the pencil lead very lightly over the paper. Pretty soon, almost like the pictures from Gram's old Polaroid camera that developed as you watched them, the writing appeared.

A + G
3360 Carter St
Maplemere M

Right away I could see I'd have a problem remembering this number because of my threes and sixes both being yellow. There seemed to be a phone number, too. I groaned as the numbers appeared one by one. Not only was it more yellow, but white ones and a zero and a couple of blank spots where I had pressed too hard: 3-661-013. A whole string of confusing white and yellow, and too many missing numbers to be useful. Still, the whole address was there. The "A & G" sort of rang a bell. I ran back into Carly's room and pulled out the note—*Find out where Alex and Grace are living now.* Okay, these must be friends she was trying to locate, maybe to stay with them. I called Tenzie.

"I found an address. I don't think Carly is going to Hollywood. It's 3360 Carter Street, Maplemere—well, it doesn't have the whole state, just M. What would that be? Mississippi, right?"

I could hear Tenzie sigh. "Or Minnesota, Missouri, Montana . . . um . . . Massachusetts, Maine, Maryland, Michigan."

"I guess there are a lot of M states," I said. "Well, can you look it up with the street address?" I gave her the partial phone number, too.

"Those should help," Tenzie said. "Go pack and get some sleep. I'll see you in the morning."

✦ ✦ ✦

When I went into the kitchen early the next morning, Gram was sitting at the table, her back to me, eating bacon and muffins and reading the paper. I stopped, thinking I should sneak out another way so she didn't see me. But I couldn't leave without saying good-bye, could I? I was still mad at her, but she had raised me, which was more than Carly had done.

Before I could decide what to do, Gram looked over her shoulder. "Help yourself to some bacon. I have a second batch of almond muffins ready to come out of the oven."

"That's okay," I said. "I'm not hungry."

Gram folded her newspaper. "Well, you're not going to school without breakfast. Why are you up so early, anyway?"

"I'm walking to school this morning." I edged along the counter, inching my way toward the door.

Gram got up, her chair scraping against the floor. "All the more reason to eat." She opened the oven, letting the delicious baking smell take over the room, and motioned for me to sit while she dumped hot, steaming muffins onto a platter. Then she split open a muffin and buttered it. I took my first mouthful and wanted to stay at that table forever. I was already questioning my decision to go off with Tenzie. She always seemed so sure of herself and ready to take risks, but I liked things to be familiar and comfortable. Maybe Gram had her reasons for keeping me here. Maybe she felt she was protecting me from Carly.

Just as I was thinking about calling Tenzie to tell her I wasn't going, the phone rang. Gram answered it. "It's for you—Tenzie."

I took the phone into my room. "Are you ready?" she asked. "Does your grandmother suspect anything?"

"Listen, Tenzie," I said, muffling my voice with my hand to keep Gram from hearing, which wasn't necessary because I couldn't get in another word.

"Oh, I knew it! You're chickening out, aren't you? I want to remind you of one thing, Basil Feeney. This is probably your last chance to live with your mother. If you let her take off now without following her, you may never find her again. Even if you did find her years from now, she probably wouldn't want to have anything to do with you."

I felt as if she had kicked me in the stomach.

"Basil, get out of there now, you hear? I'm waiting for you."

"Okay," I whispered, and hung up the phone. I rushed through the kitchen, grabbing my backpack. "Gotta go."

"Aren't you going to finish your muffin?" Gram asked.

"I'm full," I said. I didn't look back. Tenzie was right. If I didn't leave now, I might never see Carly again. I ran all the way over to Tenzie's house.

When I arrived, I found Tenzie standing in the driveway. There were two bikes leaning against the garage door. "Where did you get two bikes?" I asked.

"The red one is Dad's, and the blue one belongs to my mom."

"Don't you have your own bike?"

"I was supposed to get one for my birthday the year before last. They forgot it back then, but said I'd get it last year for sure."

"And?"

Tenzie shrugged. "They forgot about it again. But don't worry. They'll never miss these bikes. Even with the great weather in California, I never saw them ride once." She started to get on her dad's bike. "Let's get going. I looked up the schedules. If Carly missed the bus last night, she'll be boarding the ten-twenty this morning. If we hurry, we could catch her."

Suddenly I realized what a huge deal running away would be. "Wait, Tenzie. Couldn't we talk this over a little more before we go off and do something crazy?"

Tenzie got off the bike and stood facing me, her hands on her hips. "Oh, good idea, Basil. Let's stand here discussing this for the next hour or two while your mother travels farther and farther away. That makes all kinds of sense."

"But if she caught the bus last night, it's silly to go after her when we don't really know where she is."

"We have an idea where Carly is trying to go. That's the best we can do for now, and I'm going with it. Either come now, or I'm leaving without you." She went over to a cardboard carton in the garage and pulled out two bike helmets. She tossed one to me, then put the other one on her head and yanked the strap tight.

"But maybe I should just stay here . . . with Gram."

I had started that sentence loud, but Tenzie's look made me end in almost a whisper.

"I'm not even answering that." She swung her leg over and took off.

"Wait!" I yelled. "Where are we going?"

"Michigan," she called over her shoulder. Her red bike glinted in the early morning sunshine. I kind of wished I had that one instead of her mother's bike. I started to follow, but wasn't used to the fancy gears. I was madly spinning the pedals without getting anywhere. By the time I got the gears to stop grinding and start working, Tenzie had disappeared around the first curve.

When I got out to the main road, I stopped for traffic and was tempted to ride across into my own driveway and let Tenzie go on alone. I wasn't even sure how far it was from Pennsylvania to Michigan. And who knew if Carly was even there? But I could still hear Tenzie's words ringing in my head. If I didn't go now, I might never see Carly again. She wasn't perfect, but she was my real mother. As crazy as this plan sounded, I had to give it a shot.

I looked at our house and pictured Gram having a second cup of coffee while she finished the paper. Then she'd go out to the hippie room and start working. How would she feel when she knew I was gone? I couldn't think about that. I took a deep breath and plunged down the hill toward Broxburg.

✦ ✦ ✦

I pushed as hard as I could for the next half hour, up one hill and down the other side, up the next and down again. But I never did catch up to Tenzie until she stopped at the top of a long hill, leaning her bike against a tree.

She checked her watch as I pulled up, breathless from the climb. "We're going to be too late for that ten-twenty bus."

I propped my bike against the other side of the trunk. "This is a great time to figure that out. So now what do we do, go back?"

"Of course not. We'd never be able to pull this off again. Gram and my parents would be watching every move you and I made." Tenzie walked over to the edge of the road and stuck out her thumb. A car was coming up the hill.

"What are you doing?" I yelled.

"I'm getting us to Broxburg before the bus leaves,

that's what I'm doing. C'mon, Basil. They're stopping for us."

As the car pulled over just beyond us, the passenger-side window rolled down and a woman called out, "You kids need a lift?" I couldn't see the driver.

"Yes, thanks!" Tenzie called.

Was she crazy? We couldn't get into a car with strangers. "We don't know these people."

"Oh, Basil, you've been watching too many crime stories on TV. Stay here if you want, but I'm going." Tenzie ran ahead to the car, grabbed the door handle, and jumped into the backseat. She was really hitchhiking with these people! My brain kicked in fast enough to notice the license plate—blue C M yellow orange brown yellow. I whispered it to myself to help remember it to tell the police later when ... when what? When they found Tenzie's body in a ditch somewhere?

"Are you coming?" the lady called to me. I ran up to the car. Tenzie slid over to make room for me, but instead, I grabbed her arm and pulled her toward the door.

"Get out!" I said.

"Basil, stop! You're embarrassing me."

I grabbed her arm with both hands, yanked her out of the car, and slammed the door. "We don't need a ride."

"Suit yourself," the lady said. The window rolled up, and the car pulled out onto the road.

Tenzie shook loose from my grasp. "What is your problem? There goes our chance to catch the bus."

"You're the one with the problem. You have no idea what those people might have done to you. And don't even think about flagging down another car because I'm not letting you do it."

Tenzie's face was red with anger. She started to say something, then clamped her mouth shut, climbed onto her bike, and took off, her back tire spitting gravel at me as she crossed the shoulder of the road.

I started off after her, but like before, I couldn't close the gap between us. She was cranking like a racer in the Tour de France. The ride gave me some time to think about what we were doing. Tenzie had just shown me that she had no common sense whatsoever, and now I was following her on a wild goose chase to catch the mother who deliberately had left me behind twice. Even if we found Carly, would she be happy to see us?

Would we be able to talk her into coming back home? And who knew if the address I found was where she was going?

I hadn't noticed what time it was when Tenzie checked her watch and told me we were going to be late. But we hadn't stopped for long, and we'd been riding a lot faster since then. Maybe we'd be there in time for the bus after all. Maybe Carly had missed last night's bus and was still in the station.

I played all kinds of scenes in my head as I followed the shrinking figure of Tenzie down the road. In the worst one, we pulled into the station, and Carly was glad to see us, but she didn't want to go back to Gram's.

"Then we'll come with you," Tenzie says.

"Okay, but I only have enough money for one extra ticket," Carly says.

"Take me! Take me!" Tenzie singsongs in her Peter Pan voice.

"Yeah, we can't leave Tenzie here alone," I say.

Carly looks me dead in the eye. "Of course not. She's the one I'm taking with me."

"Sor-ry!" Tenzie says, batting her eyelashes at me. "Better luck next time."

The bus comes in—they both smile and get on board. A

couple of those creepy flying monkeys slip onto the bus right after Carly.

Bam! I was jerked out of my daydream when I ran over the tail of a roadkill possum because I wasn't paying attention to where I was steering my bike. It squirted stinky goop on my right sneaker. Perfect!

CHAPTER

16

When I arrived at the station, there was no sign of Tenzie. Then I saw her coming out of the door. She ran over to me. "Carly's not here, and the ten-twenty bus isn't even in yet, so we can get on it. Let's go in and get tickets."

I grabbed her arm. "Wait, how did you come up with Michigan for the address? And what if Carly is on a bus to Hollywood instead? Did you try looking up her old address online?"

"First of all, I only found Charlize LeMay, not Carly Feeney. There were six addresses for her around LA and no way to tell which was the most recent one. It doesn't matter anyway because we don't have enough money to get all the way to California."

"Okay, but how do we know that Carly is going to Michigan?"

There was a roar behind us as a bus pulled into the station. "That's our bus, Basil. I'll tell you all about it after we leave. Come on!"

There was a line at the ticket window. "Are they really going to let two kids travel by themselves?" I whispered, looking around. The only other kids there had at least one adult with them.

"They will if the kids have this." Tenzie waved a piece of paper in my face.

I batted it away. "What's that?"

"I downloaded it from the bus company's website," Tenzie said. "It's a permission slip from our parents, and it already has their signatures on it."

"But how did you get them to sign—"

"They didn't," Tenzie whispered. "I forged them. And by the way, you're my brother."

"Oh." First she tried to hitchhike, and now she forged her parents' signatures and lied about being my sister. Were we going to end up in jail before this was over? I watched a bunch of people get off the bus. Then almost everybody in the station got up and headed out to the bus to get on.

"What happens if they run out of seats?" I asked, hoping we wouldn't be able to go.

Tenzie shrugged. "I suppose we'll have to stand." The ticket line had moved along until there was only one old guy ahead of us. Then a grandmotherly-looking lady came in line behind us.

"Are we going to make it onto the bus?" she called over to the clerk.

"Don't worry, lady. You'll get on."

The old guy was taking forever to pull change out of his pocket. The lady behind us called out again, "Are you sure?"

The clerk didn't answer this time. Finally the old guy got his ticket and shuffled off toward the bus. It was our turn.

"Let me do all the talking," Tenzie whispered as she moved into place in front of the window.

"You always do," I said in not so much of a whisper. Then I grinned to fend off the look she shot at me.

"We need two tickets to Maplemere, Michigan," Tenzie said.

The ticket agent looked up. "You kids traveling alone?"

"Yes," Tenzie said.

"I need to have a parent or guardian sign a permission slip," he said.

The lady behind us started whining again. "We don't have time for all this. We're going to miss the bus." For someone who looked like a sweet little old lady, she sure could be a pain.

Tenzie held up her piece of paper. "Here's the permission slip, all signed and ready."

The clerk looked it over. "Yeah, well, I have to talk to one of your parents, because some kids just download our permission slip and forge signatures." I felt my face go hot. I pretended to be studying the timetable on the wall behind the guy, letting the colors of all those numbers float in front of my eyes like sprinkles on an ice cream cone. Did I look guilty?

"So you two have a parent or guardian here?" he repeated.

"Our mother is here," Tenzie said, "but she had to go into the ladies' room."

"Yeah, she does that a lot," I said, getting into the spirit of things.

"Can we get our tickets while we're waiting for her to come out?" Tenzie asked. "They're almost done loading the bus. I'm afraid we'll miss it."

The old lady was whining again. "Oh, for heaven's sake," she said. "I can't miss that bus."

The clerk pulled out two tickets. "I just have to talk to your mother first, and the tickets are yours for eighty-four fifty." I couldn't believe how expensive they were. Would that use up all our money?

Just then, a woman rushed out of the restroom and headed for the door.

"Mom!" Tenzie called out. The lady turned. Tenzie waved and smiled and the lady waved back.

"She's running out to the car to grab our suitcase," Tenzie said. "She's all nervous about us traveling alone to visit our dad."

The ticket agent shook his head. "Okay, I believe you. There's no time to chase after her. Here are your tickets."

Tenzie pushed four twenty-dollar bills and a five under the metal grate in the ticket window, and the clerk passed the tickets and two quarters back to her.

He stamped the permission slip and slid it to Tenzie. "Have a good trip, kids."

"Thanks, mister! Come on, Basil. We have to say good-bye to Mom." We ran for the door. The lady was nowhere in sight. We climbed up the steps and handed our tickets to the driver. We dove into a big, comfortable, overstuffed seat. This was much nicer than I had expected—a whole lot better than a school bus.

A couple minutes later, the impatient grandmother from the ticket line climbed up into the bus. As she went down the aisle, she bonked every other person in the head with her huge swinging purse. I ducked as she went by me, then watched as she clocked the guy sitting across the aisle right in the nose. He grinned at me and shook his head after she went by.

I settled back into my seat. By leaning out into the aisle a little bit, I could see the road ahead. It didn't take long to pass by the familiar landmarks of Broxburg. Soon we were out into open country, heading down the road to who knew where.

I was excited and terrified at the same time.

We rode along in silence for a while. I think we were both amazed at what we had done, at least I was. I thought about what had happened in the past twenty-four hours. I had gone from being a kid who was content to live at home with his grandmother to somebody I didn't even recognize. I tried to make sense of where we were going.

"Okay, Tenzie, how did you figure out that we should go to Michigan? There were all those other states that begin with the letter M."

"Yes, but only a few of them had a town named Maplemere. And of those, only one had an area code with a three. I just used the clues you gave me."

"So how long are we going to be on the bus?" I asked. "And when we get to the final stop, how far is it to the house where we think Carly is staying? And what if we get to this place and Carly isn't there? Did you think about that?"

"Basil, can't you just trust me?"

"Why should I trust somebody who wanted to get in the car with total strangers? Do you know what could have happened to you?"

"Do you hear yourself? You sound like a little old lady. Sometimes you have to take risks."

"Yeah, I get that, but some risks are stupid. You weren't even scared, were you?"

Tenzie was looking out her window. "How could

you possibly know if I was scared or not?" I could see her reflection in the glass, and she was scowling.

"Because I'm your friend, remember? You've told me things, like the way you put up your magic grid when you were scared in the audition. I didn't see you putting up any magic grid when that car came up."

"Okay, you're right. That was a stupid thing to do. I wasn't thinking, okay?" She dug a paperback out of her backpack and started reading. It was *Time Tracers*, a book she had read eleven times. I read it once, which was enough.

The ride gave me plenty of time to think. There were so many questions I had meant to ask Carly. Between the play rehearsals and her arguments with Gram, I never had the chance. But I'd thought about them so much since Carly arrived that I had them memorized.

#1 You and Gram fight all the time. You don't seem to like her very much. So why would you leave me with her?

#2 Were you really planning to send for me? Because after you stopped sending letters and cards, I pretty much thought you'd forgotten about me.

#3 Even if Gram said she could give me a better home than you could, didn't you ever wonder if you could have raised me better?

#4 Is that why you came home? To see how I turned out?

#5 When you first came home, were you planning on taking me back to Hollywood with you? Or did you plan to stay in Hayes Corners? Maybe get a little house where you could raise me? Or did you just want to check me out and run away again? Was that your plan all the time?

Number five was a lot of questions, but they were all about the same thing, so I counted them as one. And the biggest question, the one I probably couldn't ask even if I was reading it off a piece of paper, was

#6 How do you think I turned out? Are you proud to have me as a son?

I thought about that last one a lot.

The bus pulled out on the highway, and the scenery got flat and boring—just a farm here and there and some cows. Then we went off an exit and through a winding road to a small town. It reminded me a little bit of Broxburg. There was even a restaurant that looked a lot like Harvey's Diner next to the bus station. I caught a whiff of bacon and wished I had eaten more at home. My stomach growled.

Tenzie glanced over at me. "Are you hungry?"

My stomach must've been loud enough for her to hear. "Yeah, but I didn't pack any food."

Tenzie rummaged around by her feet and hauled her backpack onto her lap. Then she dug inside, pulling out packages wrapped in foil. "I have two sandwiches—one chicken and one ham and cheese. There are cookies, too. Sorry, I didn't have any wheat-free stuff."

I unwrapped one of the sandwiches. It was the ham and cheese. "Thanks," I said. "I'll just eat the insides. You can have my bread."

Tenzie didn't answer, but nodded. I figured she was still mad at me, but at least she was willing to share her food. She had thought of everything. There were several bottles of water and a couple of oranges—well, not really oranges, but those small tangerine things.

After we had eaten, Tenzie rolled the foil from both of our meals into a ball and tucked it into her backpack.

"It's a good thing you brought food," I said. "This way we won't have to spend any money on eating. I couldn't believe how expensive those bus tickets were. Did that use up most of your money?"

"I knew how much they were going to cost, so I wasn't surprised. I thought you'd bring your own lunch. We're out of food, but I still have money in my backpack." She started unzipping all these pockets inside the pack and pulled out little bundles of money, which she sorted on her lap into piles of ones, fives, and tens. Then she counted the bills and gathered them all into one pile. "Okay, I still have sixty-four dollars and seventy-five cents. That should be plenty."

"What do you mean that's plenty? It's not enough for bus tickets back home."

"We don't need return tickets if we're staying with Carly. I don't know about you, Basil, but I'm not going back there."

"Well, in the first place, we don't know if we're even

going to find Carly. And if we do find her, who says she's going to let us stay with her?"

"Of course she wants us to stay with her. Carly loves us. She'll be thrilled that we figured out how to find her."

I knew that if Carly had wanted us, she would've taken us with her. Or at least told us where she was going. She certainly wasn't acting like somebody who wanted to have us along. "I don't want to hurt your feelings, Tenzie, but Carly has run out on me twice, and I'm her son. I don't remember her saying anything that could make you believe she'd be glad to see us. Do you?"

Tenzie was busy tucking money into all the little zippered pockets. She rolled her eyes, not even bothering to comment. For a while, I thought she was thinking, trying to figure out how to answer me. Finally, lulled by the rocking motion of the bus, I fell asleep waiting for her to say something.

Next thing I knew, Tenzie was poking me. "Wake up, Basil. We have to switch buses here."

It was dark, and I couldn't figure out where I was, what day it was, or why I wasn't home in my bed. Then I remembered we were on our way to Michigan. "What time is it?"

Tenzie looked at her watch. "Six thirty."

"In the morning?"

"No, it's dinnertime."

We grabbed our stuff and followed the rest of the passengers off the bus. It had turned cold, and I wondered why I hadn't thought to bring my heavier jacket. After all, it wouldn't be long before fall turned into winter. But of course I knew why I hadn't brought my winter jacket. I wasn't all that sure about staying with Carly, even if she wanted us. It would depend on her answers to my questions.

Tenzie checked the schedule board. "Our next bus leaves in half an hour. That gives us just enough time to eat."

The station was a modern building with a food court, a gift shop, and a huge waiting room. We hit the restrooms, then went into the food court. Tenzie bought a hamburger for each of us and an order of fries to split. She never asked me what I wanted, but fries and a burger without the bun sounded good to me.

We were just unwrapping our burgers when the guy who'd been sitting across the aisle from us on the bus brought his tray over to our table. "You kids mind if I sit with you? I've been on the bus for so long, I think

I've forgotten how to talk. It would be nice to have a little company for a change."

"Okay." Tenzie took her backpack off the chair next to her and put it on the floor. She shot me a look that said she wasn't wild about having this stranger sit next to her. Maybe she was wising up.

The guy unwrapped a sandwich. "I boarded three days ago in LA," he said. "Well, not the same bus for the whole trip, but I've been traveling all that time. I'm going to visit my grandmother in Cincinnati."

"Long trip," I said, feeling a little sorry for the guy. He seemed lonesome.

"So are you kids visiting family?"

I just nodded and took a big bite of the burger so he couldn't expect me to talk.

The guy raised his eyebrows. He polished off his sandwich in about three bites. For somebody who said he wanted some conversation, he seemed pretty rushed to get out of there. "Well, it's been fun talking with you kids. I want to check out that gift shop, maybe find something to take to my grandmother. Have a good trip." He wadded up his napkin and sandwich wrapper and slugged down the last of his soft drink.

"Yeah, have a good trip," Tenzie echoed.

"Hey, look," he said, pointing across the room. "Isn't that what's-her-name—the singer?"

Now Tenzie was interested. "Where? Who?" She stood up to get a better view.

I stayed seated, but twisted around in my chair to look. I didn't know one singer from another and didn't really care.

"Aw, she's gone," the guy said. "It probably wasn't her anyway."

Tenzie was still swivel-necking. "Wasn't who?" she asked, but the guy was gone.

I licked the burger juice and ketchup off my fingers. "I'm going outside to walk around a little in the fresh air before we have to get on the bus," I said.

"Good idea," Tenzie said. She reached down next to her chair, then stepped back and pulled it away from the table. "Basil, I can't find my backpack."

"Uh-oh. You must have left it on the bus," I said.

"No, I'm sure I had it with me because I got the money out of it to pay for the food."

"You're right. I remember you took it off the chair and put it on the floor to make room for that guy to sit." I pulled out the other three chairs. "It has to be under here somewhere." But there was nothing under the table except a couple of wadded-up napkins and a plastic spoon.

Tenzie's eyes locked on mine. "Basil, the money! Every penny I had is in that backpack."

CHAPTER 17

"That guy who ate with us must've picked it up by mistake," I said. "He had a backpack with him on the bus—probably thought he brought it in here."

"That was no mistake," Tenzie said. "Come on. He was headed for the gift shop." We ran across the lobby, smashing into each other as we both tried to go through the narrow entrance of the shop at the same time. The place was packed. Everybody from our bus must've been in there, and from the looks of it, maybe the passengers from a couple of other buses, too.

"I'll go around to the right side," I said, "and you take the left. Keep watching the door as you do it, though. He may try to make a break for it. I'll meet you back here."

I tried to remember what the guy had been wearing. There hadn't been any bright colors. His jacket was a dull nine—brown—and I could barely picture his face. I kept pushing my way through the crowd, looking right and left. A couple of minutes later, Tenzie and I met back at the entrance. "Nothing?" I asked.

Tenzie shook her head.

"We have to report this," I said. "We'll have somebody call the police."

Tenzie stopped me. "We can't, Basil. My parents probably haven't even missed me yet, but your grandmother must have been looking for you for a couple of hours. I'm sure she's reported you missing by now, and we don't want the police to know where we are before we get to Carly. It's time to board our bus. We just have to forget it."

When we got to our gate, people were already boarding. I followed Tenzie and slipped into the seat beside her. I couldn't believe we'd been gone only eight hours and we had already been robbed.

"That's him!" Tenzie cried, pointing out the window. "Look. He has my backpack." I couldn't see, because Tenzie was climbing over me to get to the aisle. She started squeezing past passengers who were getting on. I tried to follow, but some of them were already mad from being shoved by Tenzie, so they weren't about to let me through.

I finally got outside and started toward the building, but the bus driver grabbed my arm. "Whoa! There's no time to go back in there. I'll be taking off any second."

"Did you see my . . . my, um, sister leave just a second ago?"

"Yes, and I told her the same thing. Look, you can run inside to grab your sister, but you return immediately. Got it? I have a schedule, and I can't wait for you."

"Okay, thanks." I ran for the station door. A lot of people were coming out, so I had to dodge around them to get into the building. The place had really emptied out, so it was easy to run a big loop through the food court, and one more quick search of the gift shop. I found Tenzie behind the T-shirt rack, looking frantic. I heard the bus driver blow the horn three times—loud!

"That guy is gone, Basil, and so is our money." Tenzie started to cry.

"Never mind. The bus is leaving." I took her hand, and we ran for the door.

We barely got up the bus steps before the driver stepped on the gas. We both lurched forward, then tumbled into our seats.

"We need to wise up," Tenzie said. "We're not trusting anybody else. I'm so mad at myself."

"What do you mean? You hardly said anything to the guy at the table. And he seemed nice. How would you know he was a crook?"

"I'm not talking about in the restaurant. Right here in the bus, I was practically asking him to rob me. I sat here, spreading my money all over my lap to count it. He probably knew exactly how much I had. I was so stupid!"

"There's nothing we can do, so forget it. We'll be with Carly tomorrow morning. We won't need your money then."

She nodded. "You're right. We can get along on your money for breakfast and a cab when we get there. How much did you bring with you?"

"I . . . I'm not sure. I brought all the change that I had in my savings jar."

"Just change? No bills? You'd better count it now.

We need to know how much we have." Somebody had dropped one of those cardboard boxes for carrying food in the aisle. Tenzie pointed to it. "Use that to count your change in, so you don't lose any."

I looked over my shoulder to make sure nobody was watching me before I emptied out the small plastic bag that held my change. I could already see that I didn't have enough to tempt anyone to rob me. It didn't take long to come up with a total.

"Six dollars and eighty-seven cents," I said. "I'm sorry. That's not enough for anything."

Tenzie reclined her seat a little bit, and using her jacket like a blanket, pulled it up under her chin. "That's all right. All we need to do is get to Carly, then we'll be fine."

I wasn't sure if Tenzie believed that or was just saying it to make me—and herself—feel better. I was scared. We were a long way from home and almost out of money, heading for a place where we were only guessing Carly would be. If she was there, I had a bad feeling about her reaction to having us show up with no warning.

Worst of all, Gram's face flashed through my mind. She must be worried sick about me. I had been furious at her for lying to me, but she didn't deserve the heartache I was giving her now. I looked over at Tenzie. Her eyes were closed, and even though neither of us said anything after that, I was pretty sure we were both awake, trying not to panic.

+ + +

I must have dozed off because the next thing I knew it was daylight and we were pulling into the parking lot of a big diner. It was so cold we could see our breath as we got off the bus. "Where are we?" I asked.

Tenzie was rubbing the sleep out of her eyes as she stumbled toward the diner. "I don't know."

She looked pretty grumpy, so I decided not to ask her anything else. We split up to go to the restrooms, then met back at the counter. Tenzie was already studying the menu. "We can share a Danish pastry," she said. "Do you want raspberry or strawberry?"

"Can't I get eggs? I'm starving."

Tenzie shook her head. "The Danish is the cheapest thing they have. I know it has wheat in it, but you'll have to eat it or starve."

The Danish was so sweet I could hardly swallow it. I wanted to kick myself for not bringing along some of Gram's almond flour muffins. After eating one of those, I could go four or five hours without getting hungry.

From then on, we went through small towns on back roads. We made several stops along the way, but none of them were in official bus stations. "How much farther is it to Maplemere?" I asked.

Tenzie shrugged. "I don't know. The bus schedule was in my backpack along with everything else that we need. We'll just have to wait until we hear our stop announced."

After what seemed like another couple of hours, we came to Maplemere, where the bus station was the town drugstore.

"What happens now?" I asked as soon as we were off the bus.

"We'll take a cab," Tenzie said. "Give me the address so we can ask how much it costs."

"I don't have the address. I gave it to you over the phone. Didn't you write it down?"

"Yes, I wrote it down, but it was in my backpack. Do you remember it? I think the street was named after a president."

"Okay, Washington? Jefferson? Lincoln—"

"It was Carter!" Tenzie said. "Carter Street. Now we just need the number."

The only thing I could picture in my head was that address and phone number all made up of yellow and white. "I know it starts out with yellows, maybe three of them. And then one white at the end."

"So what are the numbers for yellow and white?"

"I told you before. Yellow can be either three or six, and white can be either one or zero."

Tenzie sighed. "There's only one white, so when you picture the number, do you see a one or zero at the end?"

"Zero."

"And there are three yellows. Are they all the same number?"

"No, I think there were two threes right next to each other. And one six. I'm pretty sure it starts with the six."

Tenzie slapped me on the back. "Bingo! Let's get our cab."

"Well . . . hold on a second. I'm not positive that's the right number." But there was no stopping her. Tenzie ran over to a cab, opened the door, and leaned in. "How much would it cost to go to 6330 Carter Street?"

"Wouldn't cost you anything," the cabbie said, "because there's no such address."

Tenzie turned to me. "Do you remember the phone number?"

More white and yellow swirled through my brain, but I didn't have any sense of what order they came in. I shook my head.

"Are you sure there's no such address?" Tenzie asked the cabbie.

"Positive," he said. "The numbers on Carter only go up to four thousand."

He could have said that in the first place. I tried to picture the number. "Maybe it started with two threes." All of a sudden, I saw it. "Yes! It's 3360. How much would it cost to get there?"

"Somewhere between six and seven bucks," the cabbie said.

"Thanks anyway," I said. "We don't have that much money."

"How much do you have?" he asked.

I shrugged. Tenzie had taken over my money, so I had no idea.

"A little over three dollars, I think," Tenzie said. "I guess we can't get anywhere with that."

"That gold locket you're wearing, girlie. Is that the kind that you can put a picture inside?"

"Yes."

"Okay, I'll give you the ride for the locket. My girlfriend loves things like that. Get in."

I was surprised that Tenzie agreed so fast. "Is that real gold?" I whispered when we were on our way.

"No. I got it in the quarter machine at the supermarket. The one where you have to grab your prize with the jaws thingie."

I felt better about that. I didn't want her to lose a family heirloom. We zigzagged across town and finally turned onto Carter Street. As I watched the numbers go up, starting at 100, the empty feeling in the pit of my stomach was growing. I could tell that Tenzie was feeling just the opposite, getting more excited with each block. By the time we were up into the 3000 numbers, the houses looked pretty run-down. Some of them even had their windows boarded up. Then the cab slowed, and there it was, an old house with peeling paint and overgrown bushes in the yard.

Tenzie bounded up the front steps. I would've liked a little time to get my thoughts together, but I couldn't stop her. The porch had an old stuffed recliner with a rip across one arm. There were piled-up cardboard cartons with rags or old clothes—I couldn't tell which—spilling out of them. Tenzie had been ringing the doorbell, but nothing happened, so she knocked. All of a sudden, it sounded like a whole pack of dogs were coming to the door. One smashed into it so hard, I thought he was going to come right through. There was a window at the top of the door, and a small, yippy dog kept bouncing so high that his face would appear for a second until he dropped back to the floor.

A guy's voice yelled, "Knock it off, you mangy mutts!" When he opened the door, a huge dog started to come out, and the guy dropped him with a loud "Down!" The little dog leapfrogged the other one and came right for me. I backed up, forgetting about the steps, and landed faceup on the front sidewalk. The dog grabbed my T-shirt, snarling.

"Pixie! Get back here." When Pixie didn't let go of me, the guy came down and peeled her off me. "Sorry, dude. She doesn't like strangers coming to the door. If you kids are selling magazines or cookies or whatever, we just don't have the cash for that kind of stuff, okay? Good luck with it, though."

Tenzie had come down the steps to help me. "We're

not selling anything, mister. We're looking for Carly Feeney. Is she here?"

The guy was holding Pixie over his head, her little legs churning like a pinwheel. He went up the steps and slipped her through the door, where she started bouncing again, her pointy snout flashing in the window every few seconds.

The guy scratched his head. "Sorry, kids. I don't know anybody named Carly. You think she lives around here?"

"No, that's okay," I said. "We must have the wrong address. Thanks anyway." I turned and headed toward the street. For a few seconds, I was relieved that this was the wrong place, because it was a dump. But then the awful truth hit me. We had been wrong about our clues to follow Carly. We were in the middle of nowhere, and we didn't have enough money to get home.

CHAPTER 18

"No, wait!" Tenzie rushed up the steps. "Maybe you know Carly by a different name. Some people call her Charlize. Does that sound familiar?"

"Charlize?" He grinned and shook his head. "We know a Charlize LeMay. She never mentioned that her real name is Feeney."

"Are you Alex?" Tenzie asked.

"Yeah, that's me. So how do you know Charlize?"

Tenzie pointed at me. I couldn't have felt more threatened if she'd held a gun. I knew what she was going to say. "Charlize is Basil's mother."

"No way!" Alex started to chuckle, finally laughing so hard, he had to lean against the front door. "I mean, no offense, kid, but Charlize is a mother? That is totally messed up." He opened the door and called inside. "Hey, Grace, come down here. You gotta hear this."

Footsteps thumped down the stairs, and pretty soon Grace appeared in the doorway. She looked a little older than Carly. She had wild dark brown hair and was wearing a long skirt and ruffled blouse that reminded me of Gram's hippie clothes. "Hi, kids," she said. "What's up?"

Alex nudged her arm. "This is going to blow your mind. This is Charlize's kid."

Grace came out on the porch and looked closely at my face. "Yeah, I can see the resemblance around the eyes. Where has she been hiding you all this time? You must be, what? Eleven? Twelve?"

"Basil is twelve," Tenzie said. I wished she'd stop talking for me. "He's been living with his grandmother. Then Charlize came home and stayed for a couple of weeks."

"I can't believe it," Grace said. "I mean, how long did we know her, Alex? We met her when we first moved out to LA, and there were probably a couple of years before she moved in with us."

"How long did Carly live with you?" Tenzie asked. What was she, a detective?

"Had to be over three years," Alex said. "She was broke, so we gave her a place to crash until we left LA last month and came back here."

"Yeah, and we're not getting into that trap again, are we, Alex?" Grace gave him a look.

I was trying to do the math in my head. If Carly left home seven years ago, almost half of that time she was mooching off Alex and Grace. So coming home was probably more about being broke than wanting to see me. The more I learned about my mother, the less I wanted to live with her.

Alex and Grace were studying me like a science specimen. I felt like one of those butterflies that they smother with chloroform on a cotton ball, then pin to a display board.

"And get this," Alex said. "She wasn't even telling us the truth about her name. She's Carly Feeney. How's *Feeney* for a glamorous name?"

"It's my name, too." I wasn't hanging around for any more of this. "C'mon, Tenzie. We're out of here."

Grace reached over to touch my shoulder. "Aw, I'm sorry, kid. This just came as a surprise, you know? In all the years we knew your mother, she never said a word about you."

"Thanks a bunch for sharing that," I mumbled. I'd already gotten that message when Alex said it, and I didn't need the knife to go in a second time. I headed for the street.

"Hey, don't leave before Charlize gets back," Alex called. "She just went out for groceries. Should be back any minute."

"She's here?" Tenzie's voice rose to a squeal.

"Yeah, she got here last night needing someplace to stay—as usual." Grace held the door open. "You kids might as well come in and wait."

I wasn't going in there. "I'll stay here on the porch."

The three of them went inside while I settled on the bottom step. Whichever way Carly came from the grocery store, I'd be able to see her. I heard a crash and saw that a skinny stray dog had tipped over a bent-up metal garbage can a few houses down. He dove into it and started pulling out garbage.

It was some kind of miracle that we'd found Carly at all, but there was no way we could stay here. I couldn't believe she had never mentioned me to her friends. If she had been planning to send for me, wouldn't she have told people about that?

I had been sitting on the porch steps long enough to watch the dog eat most of the garbage he'd spilled from the can when I saw Carly coming down the block, carrying two grocery bags. She had her head down. I knew she didn't see me. I didn't want to meet her out here like this, just the two of us, so I panicked and went inside. The dogs didn't bark or attack this time—just did a lot of pretty personal sniffing.

Tenzie was sitting at the table with Grace and Alex. "Carly's not here yet?" Grace asked. "That's funny. The grocery store isn't that far away. Tenzie has been telling us that she wants to be an actress. I'm trying to talk her out of it."

The front door opened, and Carly came in. When she saw Tenzie and me, she squinted at us for a second, as if she couldn't quite figure out who we were. Then it hit her and the color drained from her face. "Basil! What are you doing here?"

Before I could open my mouth, Tenzie ran over and hugged her. "I'm so glad we found you. You left without even saying good-bye."

Carly took Tenzie by the shoulders and held her at arm's length. "Tenzie? How did you get here?" Carly turned to me. "Did my mother give you this address? No, wait, there was no way she would know it."

Tenzie reached out and took Carly's hand. "Aren't you glad to see us? We want to live with you from now on."

That's when Carly pushed Tenzie away and started freaking out. "Oh, my gosh! You two ran away! Nobody at home knows where you are."

"I'm sure my parents haven't missed me," Tenzie said. "They were gone yesterday morning before I got up. Mom had stuck a note on the refrigerator, telling me to heat up the dinner she left in the freezer. They never bother to check my room when they get home."

"Man, that's rough," Alex said. "You could go a whole day without your parents knowing you were gone?"

"Once I went three days without seeing my mom," Tenzie said.

Grace looked concerned. "You don't have a father?"

"Barely," Tenzie said. "He's so worried about his job, he stays at work for long hours."

"Stop it!" Carly shouted. "Yes, she has a father and a

mother, and she lives in a nice house. Tenzie, you have to call your parents right now."

Tenzie gripped the edge of the table. "No! I won't call them. I want to stay here with you." Didn't Tenzie get it? If Carly had wanted us to follow her, she would have sent for us.

"Maybe the kids could stay here," Alex said. "They wouldn't take up much room."

"And sleep where?" Carly yelled. "On the couch with me?" She pulled out her cell phone and handed it to Tenzie. "Here, call your parents right now, or give me the number and I will."

Tenzie put her head on her arms. "No."

I felt bad for Tenzie. It had been more important to her to find Carly than it was for me. Nobody was saying anything now. The only sound in the room came from the big dog, snoring on the couch.

"Do you have to send us back right away?" I asked.

"Basil, Tenzie's parents must have called the police by now. Since I'm the adult in this situation, I'm the one who's going to get blamed. For all I know, I could be accused of kidnapping Tenzie. Did you even think of that before you started out?"

At first I had been impressed with the way Carly

was taking charge, acting concerned about Tenzie and me getting home. Then I realized it wasn't about us at all. She was only worried about saving her own skin.

I slipped into the chair next to Tenzie and patted her shoulder. "It's going to be okay," I whispered, even though I didn't believe it. "Now your mom and dad will realize what lousy parents they've been. I bet they'll pay more attention to you after this." More lies. What was the matter with me? I sounded like one of those people who say what they think other people want to hear. My little speech didn't help anyway. Tenzie kept her face hidden. The shaking of her shoulders let me know she was crying.

Alex got himself a soda from the refrigerator and came back to sit next to me. "The kids are probably better off with you, Char—Carly. I mean, the boy is yours anyway, and it doesn't sound like the girl has much of a home life."

Tenzie lifted her head. "Please? I'll do anything you want. I can cook and clean, and Basil can . . ." She stopped there, not able to come up with anything I'm good at.

Grace stepped in. "Are you all crazy? These kids are runaways. We can't have them here. Carly, you have to send them back home." That got Tenzie crying again. Grace and I seemed to be the only two people in the room with any brains.

"Do you have any suggestions how to do that, Grace? I don't have the money for bus tickets."

"Well, if you're dropping a hint," Grace snapped, "don't be expecting us to foot the bill. Your gravy train went off the tracks a long time ago. Besides, we're broke."

"Gram would pay for my ticket," I said. "Tenzie's, too."

My mention of Gram seemed to set Carly off. She started pacing the room. "Oh, I'm sure that witch would love to see me fail again. I'm not taking a penny from her. I have to get you kids back without her help or I'll never hear the end of it."

Carly thought she had never taken a penny from Gram? What did she call the money Gram had spent all these years supporting her kid?

Alex did a slow shrug. "If you want, you could borrow the old truck in the backyard to drive the kids home. We mostly drive our VW Bug anyway."

Carly's face lit up. "There's a truck? Let me take a look at it."

"Okay." Alex reached for a set of keys on the wall

and tossed them to Carly. She went out the back door, with Tenzie following close behind.

Grace leaned over Alex's shoulder. "You can't trust her. She'll never bring it back."

"Who cares? We'll never use that thing because it burns so much gas. Besides, the registration has run out, and the head gasket is going to blow any day. We can't afford to get it back on the road. It's junk."

They were saying these things right in front of me. Did they think I was too much of an idiot to understand?

"Let's make her pay for it, then," Grace said.

Alex laughed. "With what? She's worse off than we are."

They stopped talking when Carly came back in. "That truck is pretty rusty. How long has it been since anybody drove it? Are you sure it runs?"

Grace put her hands on her hips. "Aw, we're sorry, Carly. If we'd known you were going to run off with our truck, we would have bought something newer and fancier."

Tenzie came through the door. "The truck looked fine to me, Carly. Let's take it, okay?"

Now all of a sudden Tenzie wanted to go home?

This wasn't making any sense, but I wanted to get out of there so bad, I didn't mention anything about the truck being a junker.

Tenzie was scooping Carly's clothes off the floor and shoving them into her purple suitcases. Carly started digging through the two bags of groceries on the table. "Now that I'm not going to be eating your food, there's no sense in leaving this here, except for the stuff that will go bad without a refrigerator." She pulled out a package of ground beef, a carton of ice cream, and a half gallon of milk, and set them on the table. Then she changed her mind about the milk and shoved it back in the bag.

Grace scribbled something on a piece of paper and pushed it across the table to Carly. "Sign this. I want something in writing to prove that you're taking our truck and you agree to bring it back."

"What the . . ." Alex looked puzzled.

Grace whispered to him, "It's worth a couple hundred bucks for scrap."

"Whatever." Carly scrawled her name on the bottom. Actually it could have been anybody's name—just a squiggle, like a movie star's autograph.

"Write it so it's legible," Grace said. "And add the date after it."

Carly rolled her eyes and made a big show of writing carefully. Then she tossed the truck keys in the air and caught them with a jangling flourish. "See you!" She spun around, motioned for me to grab her suitcases, and was out the door before I could move. She never thanked Grace and Alex for the truck. But I had a funny feeling that they should be thanking her for getting a big hunk of junk out of their backyard.

+ + +

Once again I found myself, stunned, sitting in a moving vehicle. Tenzie was in the middle of the seat, next to Carly, and I was pressed against the door. The seat belts were all jammed up, and the lock on the passenger door didn't work. So if Carly got us into an accident, which didn't take the slightest stretch of imagination, I would become a speeding missile, either through the windshield or out the sprung door. When I brought up the subject of safety, Carly said, "Basil, don't be such a wimp. You sound just like your grandmother." I knew she meant that as an insult, but I took it as a compliment. I'd have given anything for Gram's brand of common sense right then. She had seen through Carly years ago.

I wondered how serious it was to be driving with

an expired registration, and I didn't know what a head gasket was, but the way Alex said it, it sounded important. Still, if it was a way to get back to Gram, I was okay with taking a risk.

Tenzie was smiling and humming to herself, which made me worried that she'd gone off the deep end. She couldn't possibly be happy about going home. Then she opened her mouth, and it all became clear. "So where are we going?"

"Where do you think?" I said. "Home."

"No, I mean where are we *really* going?" Tenzie was looking up at Carly like a fan at a rock concert—the one person who didn't see through her even a little bit. After being robbed, Tenzie had said we shouldn't trust anybody. Carly seemed off-the-charts untrustworthy to me. Why couldn't Tenzie understand that?

Carly kept her eyes on the road. "Like Basil said, I'm taking you both home."

"Well, in the first place," Tenzie said, "you're Basil's mother, so he's already home. And my parents? You'd be doing them a favor if you'd take me off their hands. Really. Call them. They'll tell you."

Carly reached over and patted Tenzie's hand. "You

can't keep running away, sweetie. Your parents must be frantic."

Tenzie snorted. "Yeah, right! They're simply lost without me."

"I'm sure they are," Carly said.

"You don't even know my parents," Tenzie shot back.

"No, I really don't, but I know your mother must love you very much. I mean both of your parents must—"

"I don't believe it," Tenzie interrupted.

I had to agree with Tenzie on that one. Having somebody tell you your parents "must" love you wasn't very reassuring.

The next thing that Carly did almost knocked the wind out of me. She raised her chin, deepened her voice, and sounded as if she were delivering lines from a play. "I know how it is to be a mother, Tenzie. Every day that I was away from Basil, I thought about him, worried about him, and wondered what he was doing. I've loved him from the minute he was born, and I always will. That's the truth."

Those were the words I had waited for Carly to say since the day she left seven years ago. But now she was talking to Tenzie instead of me. And . . . wait a minute . . . weren't those lines from her TV movie? She wasn't even talking about herself and me. She was just reciting a speech that seemed to fit the situation.

At that moment, any small bit of trust I still had in Carly evaporated. I picked the words that perfectly fit the situation for me.

"Carly Feeney, you are so full of crap."

CHAPTER 19

Sometimes you can be with a person with neither of you saying anything, and it feels as comfortable as sinking into a soft, broken-in sofa. Gram and I were like that all the time, working or reading side by side, and then one of us would speak up and say just what the other person had been thinking—like mind reading.

This was not that kind of silence. Ever since I had called out Carly on her phony "mother" speech, I could almost taste the angry thoughts from Carly and Tenzie sputtering and fizzing around that truck, but not coming at me as words. Seriously. I could taste the anger—sort of metallic. Was that another part of my synesthesia?

I knew I had read something about people tasting words. I'd have to look it up. Were new weird things about me going to keep cropping up my whole life until I was so odd I would have no friends at all? Come to think of it, I only really had Tenzie as a friend, and from the stink eye she was giving me now, my friend total was back to zero.

Carly's fury showed in her driving. As she took a turn too fast, I had to brace my feet on the floor to keep from slamming into the door. I was ankle deep in fast-food wrappers, cups, and napkins, which was probably a good thing, because when I pushed the debris aside, I could see something moving. When I looked closer, I was seeing flashes of white line speeding by under a rusty hole eaten out of the floor. Before my brain could register that we were over that center line, there was a blast from a truck horn, and Carly swerved to the right, finally bumping to a stop on the shoulder.

"Idiot truck drivers," she shouted. "Think they own the road."

"Well, he did own the side he was driving on!" I yelled. "You were halfway into his lane. You almost got us killed." I knew Carly was disorganized and unreliable, but even after she had me dangling head down from the barn rafter, I had given her the benefit of the doubt. Now I saw Carly for what she really was—reckless and dangerous.

Carly sneered at me. "But we weren't killed, were we? I believe we're all breathing in here. Right, Tenzie? You're breathing?"

Tenzie giggled, but she seemed uneasy. Maybe now she'd see Carly the way I did.

Carly leaned forward so she could look around Tenzie. "And Basil must be breathing because he has enough air to criticize me. I swear you sound exactly like my mother. She has turned you into a neurotic little bundle of nerves. Instead of taking you back to her, I should carry you off to California and teach you how to live free instead of worrying about insignificant things."

"There's nothing insignificant about crashing head-on into a truck," I said. "Gram was right not to let me go off with you when I was five. I probably wouldn't have lived past the age of five and a half."

Carly had swiveled in her seat so she was leaning on her door, her left arm draped over the steering wheel. She was looking at Tenzie now. She narrowed her eyes. "I think you're right about your parents, Tenzie. If they haven't figured out what a treasure you are in . . . how old are you?"

"Eleven."

"If they haven't figured out what a treasure you are in eleven years, then they'll never see the real you." A smile crept across her face. Then she slapped the steering wheel. "You know what, kids? I'm going to rescue both of you."

Carly slid back into driving position, slammed the truck into gear, and floored the accelerator. As soon as we hit the pavement, she did a tight U-turn, overcorrected, and fishtailed us for half the length of a football field. Then she must have scared herself because she gradually calmed down and started driving like a normal person instead of a demolition derby racer. I could keep my eyes open now without being terrified. I guess that was why I had the courage to bring up the subject of calling home.

"Remember back at the house, you were going to call Tenzie's parents? Can you do it now?"

"I changed my mind about that, Basil. Even if her parents did call the police, what are the chances that they would find us? I mean, do you know how big this country is? There are a million back roads, and they have no idea what kind of vehicle we're driving. It's like finding a needle in a haystack. I know I can get you safely to California without being caught."

Was she kidding? Never mind her use of the word *safely*, which was too ridiculous to think about. Did Carly really think being on back roads would keep the police from spotting us? Hadn't she ever seen any of those manhunt TV shows? We'd be sitting ducks. But she was acting so weird, I figured I'd better humor her.

"Okay, let's not call them, then. But I really want to call Gram. I know she's worried."

Carly laughed. "Oh, she's worried, is she? Let her worry. And let Tenzie's parents worry about her for a change. It will serve them right."

"That's right, let them worry," Tenzie echoed.

I couldn't believe Tenzie didn't see another side of Carly after the driving demonstration she'd just put us through. "Carly, I mean it. I need to talk with Gram. Where's your cell phone?"

Carly whipped her head toward me, which made the car swerve a little to the left, but nobody was in the other lane this time. "We're going to get one thing straight, Basil. Now that you'll be living with me, you'll call me Mom or Mama or Mother or something besides Carly. It's disrespectful. And I make the rules. There will not be any phone calls. Is that understood?"

"It's fine with me," Tenzie said. "I never wanted to call my parents in the first place. I don't care if we never see them again."

I kept quiet because I was overruled. But the first time I could get my hands on that cell phone, I was calling Gram, whether Carly liked it or not. We drove on probably for another hour. My stomach started growling. We hadn't eaten since breakfast, and the sun had dipped low in the sky.

"I'm starving," I said. "Let's stop at one of those restaurants up ahead."

"You think I'm made of money?" Carly snapped. "Besides, we can't take a chance of somebody recognizing us. We'll pull off into that little park and eat what's in the grocery bags. And don't think we'll be staying in a motel tonight. We'll sleep in the truck."

Our meal consisted of snack foods, which actually appealed to me since we never had them at home. But after a dinner of potato chips, corn chips, cheese puffs, sandwich cookies, and snack cakes, washed down with the only nourishing thing in the meal, milk, I felt sick, and my brain was so foggy I could hardly think straight.

Sleeping in the cramped truck was no picnic. Finally I convinced Carly to let me go sleep in the truck bed. It was hard, cold metal, but it felt better to stretch out than be sitting up in the same position I'd been in all day. The next morning was the same thing. We got up, ate more snacks, and drank more of the milk, which was warm and beginning to taste funny.

I had no idea how far we had gone. I saw the names of some towns, but couldn't tell what state they were in. Carly was staying on back roads. Each time we went through a small town, I hoped somebody would recognize us. But how would they? Could our pictures be in the newspaper by now?

Around lunchtime, we pulled into a small convenience store so we could get some fresh milk. I looked through all the milk cartons in the refrigerator case, turning them around to check for the most recent date. Maybe it wouldn't go bad so fast.

I took the milk up to the cash register, where Carly was buying more potato chips. She grabbed the carton from me. "What were you doing, milking the cow?"

"I was checking the dates to get the freshest one."

Carly rolled her eyes. "You are such a little old lady."

Tenzie came to my defense this time. "That last bit of milk was nasty. It had lumps in it."

I checked the newspapers on the rack below the counter, but there wasn't any story about missing kids—us. Maybe Tenzie was right—nobody missed us.

Carly handed me the milk. "Here, take this back. It's only going to go sour like the last one."

There was a guy stocking one of the shelves by the milk case. I thought about telling him that my mother was kidnapping us. But was it really kidnapping? I mean, we could get help any time we wanted. It wasn't like she was hauling us off at gunpoint. And as mad as I was at her for not calling Gram and not taking us home, I really didn't want to get her in trouble with the police. So I didn't say anything.

After I replaced the milk, I got up front just in time to see Carly buying a two-liter bottle of soda, the cheap kind, not a brand name. Great, now we were on a diet of pure junk food. For lunch, Carly didn't bother to find a park with a picnic table. We just sat in the truck and dug into the grocery bags, everybody swigging soda out of the bottle.

Carly filled the tank, and we were on the road again.

It's funny how you can drive for miles and miles, hours and hours, and not have any idea what state you're in. I tried to picture a map of the states that were sort of clustered together near Canada—Michigan, Wisconsin, then Montana and Wyoming? Did they come before the Dakotas or after? Had we gone far enough to get across the whole state, or was this still Michigan? Wherever we were, the land was almost completely flat now. I would see something way in the distance, and it took forever to get there.

Tenzie was asking a lot of questions about where we were going and how long it would take to get to California. She wasn't sounding as eager as before. Carly finally told her to be quiet because she had a headache. After that, it was hard to stay awake. I folded up my jacket to make a pillow, leaned my head against the window, and fell asleep. It wasn't until Carly pulled to a stop in a bumpy parking lot that I was jostled awake.

"Where are we?" I asked.

"I need to check some things out," Carly said. "You two can wait for me in the library."

"How can you check things out of the library?" I asked. "You need a card to do that."

"I didn't mean that kind of checking out," Carly

said. "I have to run a few errands. You kids can pass the time by reading. You don't need a library card to do that."

"Why can't we go with you?" Tenzie asked. "I'll help you with your errands."

"No. Just get out and wait for me here."

The second we were out of the truck, Carly took off. As I watched her heading toward the center of the small town, I wondered if she was driving fast enough to get picked up for speeding. I also wondered what kind of errand she had to run. It seemed to me that food and gas were the only things we needed right now. Maybe she went to get money from an ATM. Still, it was funny she needed to leave us behind. Maybe she wanted a rest from Tenzie. I could use a little break from her myself.

Tenzie had already gone into the library, so I followed. When I saw the section with newspapers, I looked for a local paper to tell us where we were, but all they had was national newspapers like the *New York Times* and the *Wall Street Journal*. Tenzie and I hadn't made the front page of either of them, but I looked inside both, hoping to find a mention of two Pennsylvania kids who had gone missing.

I had almost finished with no luck when Tenzie came over carrying a stack of books. "I love 792.028," she said.

An image of green, brown, blue, white, and purple swirled through my head. "What, the colors?"

"No, silly. It's my favorite number in the Dewey decimal system. Acting."

"I don't think you can learn that from a book."

"I know, but I hope Carly will teach me about acting or maybe sign me up for acting classes."

"Carly's not going to have any money for that," I said.

"Okay, but she can help me get ready for auditions and take me to them."

I knew that what Tenzie was saying didn't match what was in her head. Maybe I was psychic because I could feel what she was thinking. "Tenzie, this is all a great dream, but you know none of it is going to come true. Even if we make it all the way to California, which is a real long shot, we aren't going to stay there. Carly can barely manage her own life. There's no way she could handle two kids."

"You don't know that."

"Yes, I do, and so do you."

Tenzie stared at me for a minute, then shook her head and disappeared into the stacks.

I pulled out a big road atlas. I traced how far we had gone from home to Alex and Grace's, then tried to figure out where we were now. But I didn't remember many of the towns we had gone through, so I couldn't follow our route. I played the asking-for-help argument in my head again, but decided to hold off for now. Maybe when Carly came back from her errands, I could convince her to call Gram and head for home.

For a while, I killed time sitting in the magazine and newspaper reading area at the front of the library. That's when I discovered the mailing labels on the magazines. After all the driving we had done, we were still in Michigan. Carly must have been going in circles, wasting time and gas. I was sitting next to a window where I could see cars coming from the direction of town. I started playing a game. If I looked away and counted to twenty-five in my head, the next truck would be Carly's. I did that over and over, probably fifty times, but the next truck was never hers.

Carly had dropped us at the library at two thirty. Now it was four forty-five. Where was she? I had a sinking feeling in my stomach. I looked around for

Tenzie and found her reading in the fiction section. She was sitting on the floor, leaning against the end of the shelf.

She looked up. "Is Carly here?"

"Not yet."

"It's almost five o'clock, Basil. I think something's wrong."

"That old wreck of a truck probably broke down," I said. "Maybe she tried to call us. I'll go check."

I went to the desk and waited my turn. "Excuse me. My mother's late picking me up. Did she call and leave a message for me? My name is Basil."

The librarian looked concerned. "No, I'm sorry. There haven't been any calls. Maybe she just lost track of the time. Is she very late?"

"No, not really. Thanks." I went back to Tenzie. "Carly didn't leave a message. I don't want you to freak out, but I don't think she's coming back."

"Maybe she had an accident." Tenzie looked as if she were going to cry. "She could be unconscious in a ditch somewhere."

I had to admit Tenzie might be right. There were only two reasons Carly wouldn't be calling us. One was if she couldn't, and the other was if she had taken off on us. "Okay, we need to call the police. If she's hurt or in a hospital somewhere, they would know."

"We can't do that, Basil. If she's not hurt . . . if they go looking for her and find out who she is, then she'll get arrested, and we'll never get to live with her in California. Let's hold off a little longer. She'll come back for us."

We waited another hour. Then the librarian I had talked to earlier came over to us. "Still no sign of your mother?"

"No, but it's okay," Tenzie said. "Basil forgot that she had an extra errand to do. She said she'd pick us up around seven."

The librarian looked as if she didn't quite believe what Tenzie had said. "Are you sure you're all right? There's nobody I could call for you?"

I was ready to give her Gram's number because I was pretty sure that whatever was keeping Carly from getting back to us wasn't good either way.

Then Tenzie gave her a dazzling smile. "No, everything's fine, thank you. We don't have much longer to wait."

While Tenzie read her book, I tried flipping through some magazines, but I couldn't concentrate. At seven forty-five, there was an announcement that the library was closing in fifteen minutes.

I looked out the front door. Now it was dark, so I wasn't sure I would recognize the truck if I saw it. The one thing I did spot was a pay phone across the street.

I went back and found Tenzie. "Come on."

Her face brightened. "Carly's here?"

"No. She's gone."

"Gone where?"

"I don't know, and I don't care. We're going home."

Tenzie followed me across the street to the phone. "I can't believe Carly would leave us on purpose. I thought she was my friend."

I stopped and turned to face her. "Look, Tenzie, Carly isn't a normal adult. She gets all excited about projects, but then the steam goes out of her—like directing the play or taking us to California. Gram said Carly never follows through on things."

"But she still could be hurt."

"Listen, she took off on us."

Tenzie nodded. "I know. Who are you calling?"

"Gram." I picked up the receiver, and when I heard the dial tone, I pushed zero for operator. When she answered, I said, "I don't have any money. I need to call my grandmother." She took my name and the number, then I heard the phone ringing.

"Hello?"

Just hearing Gram's voice made my throat close up. The operator asked if she would take a collect call from me, and Gram said, "Of course I will. Basil, are you all right? Is Tenzie with you?"

"Yeah, she's here, and we're fine."

Gram's voice was muffled for a second as she turned away from the phone to say something. Then a woman burst out crying. "Tenzie's parents are here. They've been worried sick about her. Where are you?"

"We're across the street from the Farber Public Library."

"Are you in Pennsylvania?"

"No. We're in Michigan."

"Michigan! What on earth are you doing there?"

"Carly has friends here, so we—"

"Carly's there? Put her on the phone."

"No, she's gone. She dropped us off at the library and said she'd be back. Now the library's closed and it's getting dark."

"The police are looking for you, Basil. You need to

call 9-1-1 as soon as you hang up. But first, get Tenzie on the phone so she can talk with her mother."

I held out the phone. "Your mother wants to talk with you."

Tenzie stepped back and shook her head.

"C'mon. You have to. Your mother's crying."

She took the phone. "Hi. . . . No, I'm fine. . . . You did? . . . I didn't think you'd notice I was gone." I could hear Tenzie's mother crying again. Tenzie had tears in her eyes. "It's okay, Mom. We're coming home."

I called 9-1-1 next. "My name is Basil Feeney. I ran away from home in Hayes Corners, Pennsylvania, and I want to go back. My friend Tenzie Verplank is here, too. There's a missing person report on us."

The woman took the spellings of my name and Tenzie's and asked where we were. Within seconds of hanging up the phone, we heard a distant siren.

We stood there without saying anything, the cold air making our puffs of breath show silver in the glow from the streetlight.

Then Tenzie whispered, "They missed me right away, Pesto. My parents actually missed me."

CHAPTER

20

When the police took me back home, Gram hugged me so hard I could barely breathe, and she didn't ask me anything about running away. But that night at dinner, she said, "I want to know everything. Lay it on me."

"We wanted to find Carly."

"We?"

"Yes, both of us." I didn't want to blame this all on Tenzie. "I never got to say good-bye to Carly."

"So you just wanted to find her, tell her good-bye, and come back home? Get real, Basil. You know I'm not buying this."

"Well, it was more than that."

"Did Carly say something to make you want to follow her?"

"No, she didn't want us to do that. We were just lucky to find the right address where she was staying."

"So if it wasn't Carly, what made you take off? Was it all Tenzie's idea?"

"Partly, yes, but it was me, too. I was mad."

"If you were mad at Carly, why did you go after her?" Gram asked.

"Who said I was mad at Carly?"

"I see." Gram looked down at her hands. "I'm the one you were mad at, right?"

I was glad she had said it instead of me. "Well, yeah, because you lied to me all those years about Carly leaving me. You never told me she wanted to take me with her."

When Gram looked up, she had tears in her eyes. "I was wrong, Basil—not wrong about keeping you here, but wrong about not telling you why, when you were old enough to understand. I realized my mistake when Carly came back home. She can be incredibly charismatic. I was afraid she'd win you over with her stories and big dreams. I think that happened with Tenzie, didn't it?"

"Yeah, pretty much."

"I'm sorry you had to see Carly and me quarreling. I shouldn't have let that happen. Sometimes she gets under my skin, but she's not a bad person, Basil. I know she loves you, and in her heart she wants to be a good mother to you, but she's just so irresponsible."

"I got a close-up view of that," I said quietly.

Gram reached over and squeezed my hand. "I guess you had to see it for yourself to understand. Are things okay between us now? I couldn't bear it if you ran off again."

A lump in my throat kept me from talking, but I squeezed her hand back.

✦ ✦ ✦

I tried to call Tenzie after dinner, but her father answered and said she was sleeping. He said the same thing the next morning and again after lunch. I told Gram about the calls. "Do you think she's grounded or something?"

"I know her parents were very upset about her running away. I'd hold off and let her call you." The call from Tenzie never came.

She wasn't in school the next day, but I finally saw her at lunch on Wednesday, at my desk-table. She looked sad, but when she saw me, she smiled and started to get up. "Sorry. I'm in your seat."

"That's okay." I slid into the chair with my back to the cafeteria, which didn't bother me as much as it used to. "I wanted to call you, but Gram said to hold off and not upset your parents. Did you hear that they canceled *Peter Pan*?"

Tenzie made room for my lunch bag and milk carton. "Yes. The girl playing Wendy called me. I tried to call you, but Dad hung up the phone. He's still really upset."

"Are your parents any different than they were before?" I asked.

"It's a little bit better. Nobody's home right after school, but Mom told her boss she had to get out at five o'clock from now on. And Dad leaves the TV station after the six o'clock weather report so we all have dinner together."

"That sounds like an improvement," I said.

Tenzie shrugged and made a face.

"What's wrong? That's what you wanted, isn't it?"

"Yes, but . . ." She sighed. "You're going to think I'm

a spoiled brat, but after dinner they each work on their computers, so I'm alone for most of the evening."

I leaned forward. "I have two things to say about that. First, *alone* is when the only other person in the house is the canary, and it's dark out, and you're eating frozen leftovers."

Tenzie ducked her head. "You're right. I'm expecting them to change too fast. What's the second thing?"

"You are definitely a spoiled brat."

Now it was my turn to duck as she stood up and tried to hit me over the head with her math book. For a couple of minutes, she was the old Tenzie—laughing. Then she sat down, and the sadness settled over her again.

"Pesto, do you miss Carly?"

I spoke without a second's thought. "Nope."

"Not even a little bit?"

I mulled it over, pictured Carly's face, and thought about what I was feeling. Did I miss her? "Nope," I said a second time.

"I do," Tenzie said. "It was exciting to be with her. I thought she was going to change my life."

"Carly can't change anybody's life. She can't even fix her own."

Tenzie nodded. "She never should have left us like that. I know she can't be trusted."

"I don't want to talk about Carly," I said. "How about coming over to my house after school today? That way you won't be alone waiting for your parents to come home."

"They won't let me, Basil. They blame you for me running away."

"Me! Didn't you tell them that running away was your idea?"

"I tried, but they couldn't understand why I would want to leave home. They don't want me to see you, not even at school."

"Wait a minute! I'm being punished for something you started?"

"I know. It's not fair, and I feel terrible about it. Trying to talk to them hasn't done any good. We'll have to wait it out."

+ + +

Waiting didn't help. A whole week went by, and the Verplanks still wouldn't let Tenzie see me. As mad as I had gotten at Tenzie while we were on the trip, I couldn't stand not being able to get together outside of school.

Today was Halloween, and I wondered what kind of crazy costume Tenzie would dream up. Would she go trick-or-treating? Nobody ever came to our house because they could hit more houses across the street in Elegant Acres.

Tenzie's birthday was in two weeks. I wanted to find a special present. I searched all over eBay, but couldn't find anything I thought she'd like. Then I came up with a great idea for something I could make. I couldn't do it alone. I'd need Gram's help, so I described it to her.

"This is a big project, Basil. How do you know Tenzie's parents would even want it in their house?"

"We'll keep it here, Gram. Tenzie can come see it whenever she wants."

Gram looked worried. "I hate to see you put so much work into this when Tenzie's parents don't want her coming over here."

"Look, I know that, but I still want to build it, just to see if I can. You and I haven't done a project together in a long time, Gram. I can do most of the work myself, if you get me started."

Gram finally gave in. She did the math to figure out how much glass we would need. "If you want twenty squares of each color, that's twelve squares from one sheet of glass, plus eight squares from a second sheet. I'm not sure I have enough on hand, especially if you want specific colors. Let's go look."

We went up to Gram's glass studio, where she stored big sheets of colored glass in a vertical file. Gram had everything I needed except for two sheets each of red and yellow. On Saturday, we went to the stained-glass store in Broxburg to get them. I had already started cutting the other colors. Well, Gram did the hardest part. She cut long strips of glass six inches by twenty-four, expertly snapping them off the large sheet. Then I did the crosscuts, making four squares from each strip. I smoothed the edges and rounded the corners with a bevel grinder. Then Gram used a drill with a water spray to make a hole in each corner of every square.

It took every spare minute of the two weeks before Tenzie's birthday to finish it, with Gram helping me the whole time. We decided to put it in the empty bedroom—the only one in the house with white walls. Gram hired a guy to come in and bolt a heavy wooden frame to the ceiling to hold the weight of the glass.

Attaching the wire and hanging it was the hardest

part and took most of the second week. When it looked just the way I wanted it to, I told Gram I was going to get Tenzie.

"I don't want you to be disappointed, Basil, but if Tenzie's parents still say she can't come over here, you have to accept that."

"It doesn't matter, Gram. I told you I wanted to build it anyway, whether Tenzie ever gets to see it or not."

That was a lie. Tenzie was the whole reason for the project, and I didn't know what I would do if she never got to come over again. My life had been just fine before I met her because I didn't know what it was like to have a friend. But now that I had gotten used to having her around, I was miserable without her. There was no way I'd ever tell her that, though.

I didn't even call ahead to say I was coming. I figured I had a better chance if I just dropped in and surprised them. Tenzie was the one who answered the door. She glanced back over her shoulder and whispered, "Basil, you can't be here. I told you, my parents are really mad at you."

"That's why I came. I need to talk to them. Are they home?"

"Yes, in the kitchen. But I really don't think—"

"Good, don't think. Thinking is highly overrated." I pushed past her and went to the kitchen.

Mr. and Mrs. Verplank were sitting at the table having coffee. Mr. Verplank stood up when he saw me come in. "Why are you here? Tenzie isn't allowed to have anything to do with you. You're a bad influence on her."

I didn't try to change his mind about me. "I'm really sorry, Mr. Verplank. Nothing like that will ever happen again. I promise. But Gram and I made a birthday present for Tenzie. Could she come over to our house and see it now?"

Mr. Verplank's face was turning red. "Are you listening? Tenzie can't see you at all. And that's final."

Mrs. Verplank stood up and put her hands on her husband's shoulders. "Howard, Basil and Tenzie have been good friends, and friends don't come along very often. Let her go."

"Thanks, Mrs. Verplank," I said, grabbing Tenzie's hand before her father could say anything. "You won't regret this."

Tenzie and I ran almost all the way out to the main road before we had to stop to catch our breath.

"I can't believe my parents let me escape," she said, laughing. "Is there a real present or did you just say that to spring me out of there?"

"Oh, it's real," I said. "And I think you're going to like it."

CHAPTER 21

Gram hugged Tenzie as soon as she came through the door. "It's wonderful to have you here again," she said. "Did Basil tell you about your present?"

"I didn't say what it is, Gram. We have to blindfold her. I don't want her to see it until she's all the way into the room." Gram used one of her scarves to tie over Tenzie's eyes.

"No fair peeking," I said as I led Tenzie toward the spare room. I had her sit on the floor, cross-legged, and I sat next to her. The sun had come through the picture window just in time to make the squares of colored glass glow. There were ten rows of ten squares each, starting with blue on the bottom, then blue-green, then shading all the way up through the rainbow to red, with purple at the top. The glass squares were around three sides, so we were surrounded by color, and it looked as if the whole thing was floating. Even though I had made it, the sight almost took my breath away, making my brain vibrate with numbers and colors.

"What is it, Basil? I feel like I can almost see it through your eyes. It's bright colors, isn't it?"

She was reading my mind again. I reached over and untied the blindfold.

When Tenzie opened her eyes, she gasped. She didn't say anything at first. She kept looking up and down the rows.

"You know what it is, don't you?" I asked.

It took her a minute to answer. "Of course. It's my magic grid," she whispered. "It's perfect." As she turned toward me, I could see the bright squares of light reflected in her eyes. "Pesto, this is the nicest thing anybody has ever done for me in my whole life."

✦ ✦ ✦

That night I got an e-mail from Carly, sent from her phone. I almost didn't open it, but I couldn't resist finding out what she had to say.

> Hi, Basil!!!!!!
> If you're reading this, you must be home. I purposely left you in a safe place where you wouldn't have any trouble getting back. I just couldn't bring myself to say good-bye in person. I'm still driving across the country, but this old truck is a piece of junk. No way I'm driving it all the way back to Grace and Alex. As soon as I get settled in a place of my own and get lined up with work, I'll send for you. I hope Tenzie understands that I can't have her here, at least not while she's a minor. But you're my son, and it's my responsibility to raise you. I can't wait until you're out here. You and I are going to have a wonderful time together.
> XOXO Mom
> P.S. I like the sound of Mom, don't you?

I stared at that e-mail for quite a while. How typical of Carly to think she could solve everything by dashing off an e-mail. It would take a ten-page handwritten letter for all the things we needed to say to each other.

I hit Reply and typed, "Have a nice life, Carly."

My finger hovered over Send for several minutes, but I didn't push it. Carly couldn't help being the way she was. Gram saw the good side of her, even though they had been arguing with each other for years. I hit Delete twice—once to get rid of my reply and once to throw Carly's e-mail in the trash.

Click. Click. Gone.

Maybe Gram was right about Carly wanting to be a good mother, but I couldn't wait around until she got her act together. Gram was my rock, and the best thing that ever happened to me. She was all the mother I needed for now.

I dug into the back of my closet and pulled out Gram's game cabinet. In all the confusion Carly caused, I had forgotten about it. Gram and I had only played Truth Detector twice, and she trounced me both times. I set up the game cabinet in the hippie room and shouted up to the loft, "Hey, Gram. You want to come down and play a game of Truth Detector?"

"You think you can win this time?" she called back.

"Absolutely!" I yelled back. And to myself I said, "I already have."

WHICH IS ORANGE—
TUESDAY OR WEDNESDAY?

A Conversation Between MJ Auch and Her Editor,
Fellow Synesthete Christy Ottaviano

Sometime in December of 1999, I got a startling call from my friend, author Vivian Vande Velde. "You know that weird thing you have with colors and numbers? There's an article about it in *Discover Magazine*. It's called synesthesia." Vivian knew about my numbers/colors weirdness because of my difficulty in remembering phone numbers. I could remember the colors in the phone number, but never the order.

Vivian's call opened a whole new world for me. I had associated colors with numbers and letters my whole life, but now it had a name and I was part of an elite group called synesthetes. I once had a phone interview by a researcher at NIH [National Institutes of Health] who asked a lot of strange questions, like, "When you hear a truck go by, do you smell bacon?" This let me know that the symptoms of synesthesia vary widely from person to person, and mine was a pretty mild case.

In the process of writing *One Plus One Equals Blue*, I discovered that my editor, Christy Ottaviano, is also a synesthete. So Christy and I decided to question each other to find our similarities and differences. Here's how our conversation went:

CO: How old were you when you first realized that you were seeing colors with numbers? Did you have an "Aha!" moment or was it more a slow process of discovery? When did you become aware that this ability was unique and that most people did not have your gift?

MJA: I have seen numbers as colors for as long as I can remember. All of the vowels and some consonants also had colors for me. I never mentioned it to anybody as a child, and I didn't think of it as a gift. I thought I must have had counting and alphabet books when I was little that had colored numbers and letters.

CO: I have synesthesia in a slightly different way than you; I see colors with certain words. For instance, my days of the week are all color-coded: Monday is kelly green; Tuesday is a dark green/teal; Wednesday is orange; Thursday is also green but more in the loden family; Friday is blue; Saturday is yellow; and Sunday is white.

MJA: Are you kidding? Tuesday is orange! I knew that when I was about four years old. Tuesday was orange, my least favorite color. I thought this was because my father had to work the Tuesday evening shift at his drugstore, and I didn't like it when he wasn't home. I gradually realized that all of the days had colors for me. Here are mine: Monday is red; Tuesday is orange; Wednesday is ultramarine blue; Thursday is kelly green; Friday is chocolate brown; Saturday and Sunday are both white. At least we agree on Sunday.

CO: All my life I have seen specific words almost like color-coded Monopoly Real Estate cards—Baltic and Mediterranean Avenue being dark purple; St. Charles Place and the others in that monopoly as a lighter purple; and so on. In their own way, these color/word associations seem to bring a visual sense of order to my world.

MJA: Monopoly! Now you're talking my language. I always loved the game visually because of the clear, strong colors of the cards, but I found it disturbing that they weren't in the order of the rainbow. I always arranged my property cards in rainbow order, which hindered me in playing the game because it put them out of order for their monetary value. I didn't like Connecticut, Vermont, and Oriental Avenues because they were light blue and didn't fit with the value (light and dark) and saturation of the other property cards. These are pretty sophisticated color concepts that I understood from a very young age.

CO: How has synesthesia influenced your life as a writer and an artist? In addition to writing and illustrating, you are creative in so many other ways (music, knitting, sculpture). Can you discuss some of your other creative outlets and how they are enhanced by your synesthesia?

MJA: My synesthesia has always helped me with color theory. I'm fascinated by how one color gradually shades into the next on the color wheel. In my college color theory course, we had to create color charts by arranging 40 to 50 preprinted color chips in order of hue, value, and chroma. Some thought it was tedious, but I found it comforting, relaxing, and satisfying to choose the perfect color chip to fill each space.

This skill came into play when I designed color combinations for textile prints. I had to mix paint to perfectly match fabric samples. Later, I had a job as a "zit zapper" in a school picture factory. This required instant recognition of the colors in various skin tones so I could match them with dyes to cover the zits as the pictures moved down a conveyor belt.

In music, I enjoy vocal harmony and have sung in a women's quartet. Like color shading, this involves constant small adjustments in pitch to fit your note into the chord. Synesthesia has influenced my writing in using metaphors and similes—relating two things that cross sensory lines.

How about you? Editing requires as much, if not more, creativity as writing and illustrating. Has your synesthesia helped you in your work?

CO: My synesthesia has been helpful to me from an artistic standpoint. I'm a very visual person and have always been able to create vivid mental pictures of my thoughts and ideas.

MJA: Has your synesthesia ever been a hindrance in some area of your life?

CO: Before I understood what was going on inside my head, I felt incredibly different from my peers. I kept my secret from family and friends for fear that I would be seen as a freak. I remember first becoming aware of my sixth sense when I was about ten years old. It wasn't until I was older, in college, that I realized what an asset this ability was for me. In many ways, my form of synesthesia seems linked to my appreciation for language, art, and music. I often feel I have a heightened awareness in these areas because of my synesthesia.

MJA: I had the advantage of being thought of as an artist from a young age. Artists were supposed to be weird, so I wasn't afraid of being different. I don't think I ever mentioned the number/color thing to anybody though. When you say you "see" colors, can you describe how that works? This is the thing that's hardest for me to explain to others.

CO: When I read or hear certain words, I see them in my mind in colors, so, for instance, the word *January* is always dark purple. It's a bit random in terms of which words trigger this sensation. Sometimes they are common words that I see and hear on a daily basis, like the days of the week, but other times the words might be in groupings, like the name of a movie or a book or a song. My strongest memories are also triggered by colors.

MJA: For me it's a quick impression of color. It's like watching the shower of stars. You see shooting stars out of the corner of your eye rather than looking directly at them. We frequently have writers' lunches in our area. One day a writer friend brought a poem and asked if anybody could tell what limitation she had put on herself while writing it. I knew I wouldn't be the one to figure it out because poetry isn't my thing. The others at the table were analyzing rhyme and meter. But when the poem was put in front of me, I said, "There's no yellow. There are no *E*s." This was an instant impression. If I had worked at studying the poem, I would have missed it.

The more synesthetes I meet, the more I'm intrigued by how different we are from each other. I was once at a table of ten illustrators and six of us had synesthesia. None of us agreed on the color for any number. I gave Basil my color/number system, including the flaw of having yellow for both three and six, and white for both one and zero. I made one substitution—the number two is not blue for me. But if I hadn't changed it, the title of the book would be *One Plus One Equals Magenta*, which simply doesn't have the right ring to it!